# DeLightful Parables
# for Heart & Mind

# DeLightful Parables for Heart & Mind

## by
### Irene Zahn

*The first German Original was published in March **2015** under the title:*

## *"Die Rückkehr der Einhörner"*

*The first English Edition was published as an E-Book in 2017 under the title:*

## *"The Return of the Unicorns"*

*This English Edition (2024) presents many new stories that have not been published before.*

*Translation from the German Original by the Author*

*Cover Illustration: © PanterMedia / frenta*

*Publisher: BoD – Books on Demand GmbH, In de Tarpen 42, 22848 Norderstedt/Germany*

*Print: Libri Plureos GmbH, Friedensallee 273, 22763 Hamburg/Germany*

*ISBN 978-3-7568-4227-8*

*∞ Dem Wahren, Schönen, Guten ∞*

*True beauty lies WITHIN*

*Light or Dark? Love or Selfishness? Truthfulness or Hypocrisy? Self or Selfie? Those are choices, that all of us are faced with again and again, throughout our lives.*

*Follow the adventures of the heroines and heroes in these parables, dealing with the difficulties and opportunities that arise along their paths. How they learn to distinguish between their true Self and the false Self, forced upon them by the misguided societies, whence they came.*

*And how they find their life purpose, aided in their quest by unicorns, angels, fairies and dwarfs, but also by friendly aliens from distant worlds and other benevolent guides.*

# The Dignity of a Rose

*There was once a young rose. When it was time for her to come into bloom, she unfolded her petals in a display of color and fragrance, that was second to none.*

*Everyday, she stretched towards the sunlight, drinking its friendly energy and enjoying her life. She had lots of visitors – bees, butterflies, even people – who were delighted and pleased by her beauty and gifts.*

*One day, however, a pitch-black crow came along, stood in front of the rose, who towered above it, and began to insult her:*

*'Don't show off like that! You seem to think, you were something special! You know, there is a saying: "Be humble and pure like the violet in the moss – not proud like the rose, always seeking to be admired."'*

*The rose replied amazed: 'But I am a rose – not a violet!'*

*'Who do you think, you are?' the crow scolded, annoyed. 'Well, you will see, where this will get you: "Pride comes before a fall!"'*

*Outraged, it flew away. The rose stayed behind, disturbed and shaken.*

*For quite some time, she pondered over this conversation. Could the crow be right?*

Did the rose feel superior to others? The accusations kept haunting her well into the night and she began to feel ashamed.

The next morning, she woke up contrite and crumpled and did not dare to unfold her petals. She also furled her green side leaves, to take up less space.

When the crow came by again, it stalked complacently around the rose, who was looking like a picture of misery now.

'See? I told you so: "Pride comes before a fall!" Serves you right!'

The rose slumped even more. She was almost unrecognizable and felt inferior and small.

Her guests, whom she had always delighted, didn't notice her at first, because she had changed so much. But finally it dawned on a faithful bee, that something was wrong.

She approached the unfortunate rose, looked at her attentively, and finally recognized her hostess, after all.

'My goodness, what happened to you?' the bee asked with compassion, and examined her closely, to find out, whether she was infested with parasites. But outwardly, everything was fine.

'I really didn't mean to be arrogant,' the rose sobbed.

'Whatever gave you that idea?' the bee inquired, surprised.

Thus, the troubled rose told the bee about the conversation with the crow, which had demanded, that she be humble like the violet in the moss – and not proud like a rose!

'Well, being humble is not the same as being crumpled!' the bee replied, baffled. 'You are not a violet – you are a rose! So you don't have to behave like a violet.

It is not arrogant or immodest to be yourself! You can only be happy or make others happy, if you show and gift the world with, whatever makes you special. Nobody knows, what that is, as well as you do.

Let people babble, and don't pay attention to those, who don't have your best interests at heart. You don't even know, if the crow was not merely jealous of your beauty. Maybe it was just having a bad day. It does not matter.

You are a rose! Your gifts to the world are your magnificent bloom and your wonderful fragrance.

Feel free, to show the world, who and what you are! Enjoy your life and radiate your joy – that is the greatest fulfillment in life.

Don't worry about those, who don't understand these things. Your friends are the ones, who perceive and appreciate your beauty - you don't have to pay attention to anyone else!'

The rose sighed with relief and dried her tears. Gradually she unfolded her petals and also unfurled her side leaves again. She felt a huge burden lift from her heart.

'That's better!' the bee buzzed, satisfied, and settled down on the rose.

'Thank you, dear friend, for your precious advice,' the rose responded, with a last sigh of relief.

She was determined, to only listen to her own heart from now on, and not to any blabbermouth, just happening to come along.

# The Toothless Dragon

Some time ago, in a distant land, there lived a little dragon, who had no teeth. Because every time, he had contradicted the adult dragons, and had been severely punished for it, he had – strangely enough – always lost a tooth, until he just had no more in his mouth. A shame, for such a belligerent animal as a dragon!

The other dragons mocked him: 'Aren't you a funny dragon? You can't even bite properly!'

And therefore, the other dragon children didn't let him join in their games anymore, either. His parents felt ashamed of him.

When they grew up, the young dragons were taught, how to collect and hoard treasures. Our dragon, however, was quite clumsy in doing so: Everything fell out of his mouth, because he could not hold on to it, having no teeth. He was also ridiculed by the others, when he breathed fire, since he could not direct the flame without teeth. So he soon gave up any attempt to learn it.

Another problem arose, when they hunted together: How was he supposed to get hold of an animal, if he couldn't bite?

Of course, he also stood out at the meals, since he could not eat meat, and only lived on plants that he could grind with his jaws. And while the others only went hunting every few days, he had to go searching for food all the time, since he needed a lot more plants to feed himself sufficiently, than if he could have eaten meat. Most of the time, he went out alone, because the others were busy elsewhere, when they were not hunting.

And while the other young dragons gradually learned all the skills, that a dragon must master, in order to get along in the world, the toothless dragon withdrew more and more, for no one wanted to have anything to do with him, because he was so different. Often, he cried himself to sleep.

Since he could not defend himself, the other dragons had fun teasing him, until he lashed out and bit them. Then they laughed at him, because they knew, that he could not harm them. Moreover, they were many and he was alone. He was hopelessly outnumbered.

Thus, the toothless dragon grew up, becoming shy and reserved. He no longer trusted anyone, having been disappointed far too often.

When he came of age, he ventured out into the world, far away from his own kind. The animals and people, he met on the way, initially had great respect for him, because he seemed to be so big and strong. But they soon realized, that they needed not fear him.

*Many appreciated his friendly, quiet nature, but none of them really took him seriously.*

*One day, he happened to pass by a blacksmith's workshop. The master was working on a red-hot piece of metal. With a bellows, he tried to keep a fire going, at the same time. When he saw the dragon pass by, he had an idea.*

*'Would you like to be my apprentice? I could use someone like you!' he addressed him.*

*No one had ever said anything like that to the dragon before. Insecurely and shy, he asked: 'Are you serious?'*

*'Yes, of course!' the blacksmith exclaimed. 'You are a dragon, after all! You can breathe fire, can't you? If you are skilled, you could keep the metal glowing while I work on it, and I wouldn't have to worry about the fire, in addition.'*

*'I don't think, I can do it,' the dragon hesitated, 'I never learned.'*

*'Nonsense!' the blacksmith objected. 'Let's just try it!'*

*And he showed him, where he needed the flame. The first time, the dragon tried, he didn't quite dare, and the little flame that came out of his mouth was barely perceptible.*

*'You have to blow harder!' the blacksmith shouted.*

The second attempt was a disaster. The dragon did-breath harder, but he could not direct the flame, and almost singed the blacksmith's hands.

Dismayed, he turned away and felt terribly ashamed. But the blacksmith did not give up. He took the dragon outside the workshop, and pointed to a pole:

'We have to practice this: Try to aim at this pole.'

But the dragon would not succeed – neither the next time, nor during the following attempts. The fire would always come out of his mouth, everywhere – not only in front.

People passing by stopped, watched the strange spectacle and laughed.

'What are you laughing at?' the blacksmith scolded. 'Can you do better?'

The dragon was surprised: Someone was standing up for him! Someone, who hardly knew him!

Thus, the dragon came to trust the blacksmith.

The blacksmith shooed away the unwelcome onlookers, and they continued to practice.

Until the blacksmith had an idea: 'Maybe it would work, if you curled your tongue at the sides and directed the jet of fire that way,' he suggested.

The dragon did, creating a flame, that was aimed directly at the pole. Both cheered.

'It works!' the blacksmith exclaimed. 'I am so proud of you!'

The dragon was overwhelmed. This feeling was totally unfamiliar to him: He was embarrassed, but at the same time, proud and happy.

And so he stayed with the blacksmith as an apprentice, and soon as his assistant. They became a wonderful team: The dragon breathed his fire, and became better and better at keeping the workpieces glowing, so that the blacksmith could work on them. This way, the blacksmith saved a lot of time, could accept more orders than before, and the two of them were doing well.

One day, when the dragon was on his lunch break, and enjoying a sunbath in the courtyard, a group of children passed by. The cheekiest of them, pointed at the dragon and shouted:

'Who's afraid of a dragon like that? He doesn't even have teeth!'

The others laughed. The dragon retreated into the house, very much ashamed. The blacksmith, who had overheard the exchange, told him:

'My friend, you are a great and powerful being. You have to show them, who you really are! If you duck out, they will never have respect for you.'

'How am I supposed to do that? It is true, after all, that I don't have any teeth,' the dragon sighed.

'The next time, someone comes at you like that, spread your mighty wings. And if that is not enough, breathe fire. Show yourself!' the blacksmith encouraged him.

And that is, what happened. The next time the naughty boy and his entourage taunted him, the dragon rose to his full height, spread his wings and let out a bloodcurdling scream. The children took to their heels, and disappeared in next to no time. The dragon was surprised: That had not been all that hard.

'Those won't be back, anytime soon!' the blacksmith laughed - and he ended up being right.

Nevertheless, the dragon felt miserable, because he did not consider himself a true dragon. Such a powerful animal without teeth – just imagine!

So the blacksmith came up with the idea of simply forging a set of teeth for the dragon. He took his measurements, and in the evenings, when all the other work was done, he puttered around, until he had crafted a magnificent set of teeth. This, he gave to the dragon, who shed a few huge dragon tears, moved.

It turned out, however, that the dragon did not know, how to handle it – after all, he had not had any teeth since childhood. So the first thing he did was, bite his tongue hard. This hurt and even bled.

The new set of teeth felt like an alien element in his mouth, and like a tool, he was not familiar with. Also, he didn't want to hurt anyone or go hunting, as was the way of dragons.

So the blacksmith asked him: 'What did you want teeth for, when you were a child? What could you have done better with them?'

'Well,' the dragon said, 'I could never collect treasures, like the others, or go hunting, and when I breathed fire, I couldn't direct the flame. Besides, no one took me seriously as a toothless dragon.'

'Do you think, you still need teeth for that today?' the blacksmith inquired. 'You are big and strong now! If you don't make yourself small, but show yourself as you are, everyone will give you the respect you deserve.

You can also direct the flame with your tongue, we know that, and the kind of treasures, that dragons collect, are stolen from others. Your treasure is your good heart, which is, why you don't want to go hunting, either. So - what do you need teeth for?'

This made the dragon reconsider, and he took the set of teeth out of his mouth again. From then on, he accepted his toothlessness. Perhaps he was even a little proud of it, because it made him unique.

Therefore, the dragon learned far more from the blacksmith, than just to breathe fire.

*For the first time in his life, he experienced, what it meant, to be accepted and appreciated.*

*Thus, through the love of the blacksmith, the outwardly large and strong dragon, also became a large and strong dragon inwardly, who knew, how to defend himself, despite of his gentleness. At long last, the people and animals around him, took him seriously, even though they did not need to fear him.*

*After many wonderful years together, the blacksmith died, for a human life only lasts a fraction of a dragon's lifetime.*

*The dragon, after careful consideration, returned to his homeland. And because he had travelled so much in the world, and was so wise and understanding, he was not only kindly received by the other dragons, but was soon elected their chief, for his weapons were not his sharp teeth, but his sharp mind. This impressed everyone very much.*

*Also, he had a compassionate heart and stood up for the disadvantaged, since he himself had experienced, what it was like, not to belong, after all.*

*Thus, he happily lived with his own kind for many, many years and eventually died old and full of days.*

# Ella's Quest for Freedom

Once upon a time, there was a young locomotive named Ella, who dreamed of experiencing adventures off the beaten track. She imagined, how she would get to know new interesting countries and people, and would finally be able to go, wherever she wanted to go.

When she sauntered along the seaside on her tracks, she felt an irrepressible longing to glide on the water to unknown, far-off continents, as free as the ships.

But when she told the old locomotives in the depot about it in the evenings, they only huffed, and did not understand her.

'Locomotives always run on tracks – that's just the way it is! Period!' they would say gruffly. 'Those are pipe dreams!'

But the locomotive Ella was not satisfied with always rolling along the same well-worn tracks. She wanted to be free!

A very dusty, wise old locomotive, who had seen and been around a lot in her life, overheard these conversations. One day she took Ella aside and whispered:

'I understand you. You know, the meaning of our lives is to serve each other in love. For you, this means, taking people and cargo from one place to another. That is your purpose. Only if you fulfill your purpose, can you become happy. And yet, there is a way to make your dream of freedom come true.'

The young locomotive got all excited: 'How?'

'You have to go to the Great Magiolo in a full moon night. He lives in a cave near the seaside, and can grant you any sincere wish. But think about it twice, because then you will have to leave everything you know behind, and will never be able to be happy again back home.'

Ella's heart leapt for joy. But she was also a bit anxious. And yet, she could think of nothing else over the next few days, but fulfilling her heart's desire. She had soon made up her mind, but she told no one about it.

The day before the full moon, for the first time, she did not show up for duty at the station. She had to cover a great distance to the cave of the Great Magiolo and she wanted to be there in time under any circumstances. Therefore she set off towards the sea early in the morning, even before the others were awake. The wise old locomotive had described the route to her in detail.

Ella was utterly oblivious to the heat of the day and the mountains that had to be overcome. No obstacle could now keep her from fulfilling her dream.

When night fell and the full moon rose, she had reached the cave. In front of it, a strangely dressed man was sitting at a campfire, smoking a pipe.

Bashfully, the locomotive asked him, if he was the Great Magiolo.

He looked at her with a piercing glance, as if he could see to the bottom of her soul:

'So, you want to learn about freedom? Are you ready then, to leave everything behind that is familiar to you?'

'What do you mean?' Ella inquired, a little startled.

'You need to be aware,' he replied, 'that there is no way back to your old life, if I grant you your wish. Are you sure, that this is, what you really want?'

The young locomotive gulped. But then she answered boldly:

'I want to cruise the oceans to the end of the world, moving about as freely as the ships.'

'Your wish shall be granted,' the Great Magiolo said. 'From now on, you may do your duty as a ship.'

The Great Magiolo closed his eyes for a moment, and instantly, Ella found herself as a ship in the nearby harbor. The place was a hive of activity. Busily, she was loaded with all kinds of goods and many people of all sorts went on board, as well.

Shortly afterwards, she left the harbor and was amazed at the vastness of the sea. She soon got used to her new shape, and enjoyed the wind and the waves, the sky and the stars. She felt unbound and free, although – naturally – she still had to maintain her course, but she was no longer constrained by tracks and there were many new things to learn and to discover. Ella was happy.

For many months, she now sailed the seas, got to know many a harbor, and continued to transport people and cargo, fulfilling her life purpose. Only very rarely did she look back upon her life as a locomotive and the things, that she had left behind. It seemed like a distant dream.

But eventually, she got used to her life as a ship, and more and more often she caught herself, looking up at the sky, towards the airplanes flying overhead, and she thought longingly:

'How free I could be up there - then I would not be tied to the surface anymore, wouldn't have to evade cliffs and reefs, and could view the whole world from above.'

Thus, she returned to Magiolo, as soon as she could, and made a new request:

'I want to be as free as the airplanes that can fly around the earth, without being impeded by any obstacles.'

*Magiolo granted her this wish, as well. From then on, she transported people and cargo at lofty heights. She squeaked with pleasure, when she took off as an airplane for the first time. How much freedom she now had – the sky was the limit!*

*Even though there were turbulences and thunderstorms at times, that almost made her dizzy - most of the time, she enjoyed the view, which was much wider than that, which she had experienced as a ship. Now she even reached the most remote regions of the earth, where she would never have been able to go as a ship.*

*Time flew by. Nevertheless, she sometimes found herself looking up at the stars, where she could see all those satellites and rockets, flying much higher and farther, than she could fly herself. An irrepressible longing gripped her, to travel through outer space, exploring alien beings and far-off galaxies.*

*This time, when Ella returned to Magiolo, and told him of her longing, she asked, almost in despair:*

*'Will this never end? Whenever you granted me a wish, the longing for freedom came back and the happiness didn't last very long. I always come up against limits. When will I reach my goal, and be free and happy?'*

*Magiolo looked at her lovingly: 'Never stop dreaming! As long as you can dream, you are alive. There are no limits, except those of your imagination.*

*What you can imagine, can become reality, if you wish for it with all your heart. You are a free spirit, and have not only left your tracks behind, but also, little by little, the mental restrictions, which retain many of your kind in their often unsatisfactory lives.*

*From now on, you may travel through the vastness of space, as a spacecraft. Out there, new possibilities and realities will be open to you and your path will not have any final point or limit. Your development will go on and on. You are never done. And yet, the path will bring you an unprecedented fulfillment, as long as you follow your dreams, and let no one dissuade you from manifesting them.'*

*'So, is the journey the destination, after all, as some assume?' Ella inquired.*

*The meaning of life is, indeed, to walk your path and gain new experiences,' Magiolo replied. 'Not until you have become One again with the Source of All That Is, will you have reached your goal, and will your longing be satisfied.'*

*Thus, Ella, the locomotive, expanded her horizon upwards to the stars. Should you ever observe a particularly bright shooting star in the night sky, it could be Ella, visiting her old home again, only to set off once more, to conquer new frontiers.*

# An Amazing Outing into Outer Space

*There was once a little boy, named Benedict, whose most burning desire it was, to travel through outer space one day.*

*At night, when everyone was asleep and everything was quiet, he would step up to his window and gaze longingly at the stars. For hours and hours, he would stand there. He always had a hard time breaking away from that marvelous sight.*

*During the day, he studied star maps, read books about space adventures and watched science fiction films. He was also interested in the search for extra-terrestrial intelligence and in UFOs. Everybody considered him a dreamer and a fool.*

*One night, he stood at his window again, and gazed into the sky. It was full moon. Was it full moon? In the clear starry sky, he saw a bright shining orb. But was that really the moon? It looked very strange. He observed it more carefully.*

*Was he mistaken, or did the orb move? No, that was impossible! But it was indeed moving – its position changed, compared to the stars in the background. The orb came closer and closer.*

*Finally, it hovered directly in front of his window. Benedict stepped back, startled. The orb effortlessly* penetrated the window and hovered above the window sill.

'Hello, Benedict!' he heard a voice in his head.

Benedict took a closer look at the orb. 'Is that you?' he asked, surprised.

'Yes,' the answer came back.

'Are you somebody?' he inquired.

'Yes,' he heard again.

'Who are you?' Benedict wanted to know.

He felt somewhat uneasy.

'I have come from the constellation, you call Orion. My planet is part of the star system Rigel – you know it, don't you?' the orb communicated.

'I don't believe it!' Benedict thought bewildered, but also a little curious. 'That would mean, this is an extraterrestrial!'

'You could put it that way,' the orb of light, who read his mind, answered.

'What's your name?' Benedict asked aloud.

'We don't use names, like you do. We recognize each other by our personalities and communicate directly, just like you and I do, right now. So there is no need for names. But if it helps you, you may call me "Olep",' the orb offered.

'Why do you speak English? That is very strange,' Benedict doubted him.

'I don't!' was the answer. 'I communicate without words. You yourself translate the thought impressions into your language.'

'Wow! There really are extraterrestrials!' Benedict exclaimed. 'How come, we haven't discovered you, yet?'

'Because you are searching for extraterrestrial life with inappropriate means, and you have a very limited concept, of what it might look like. You think, it would have to be material in your sense, or maybe even carbon-based. So you miss it, because it doesn't meet your expectations.

Besides, Rigel is about 770 light years away from your Earth, which means, that even if we were to respond to your signals in a way, that you could understand, you wouldn't live to receive the answer, given your short lifespan,' Benedict heard the voice in his head say.

'Is there more life on other planets?' Benedict inquired.

'Of course!' Olep answered. 'Even on Earth, there have at all times been extraterrestrials around. But since you humans can only perceive a very small segment of the light spectrum, you don't see them. They are among you, unrecognized!'

'If the Earth-people knew of this,' Benedict mused, 'they would probably be quite scared.'

'There is no need to be concerned,' Olep replied. 'Since extraterrestrials, who come to Earth, are more advanced, than you humans, and have progressed far beyond the belligerent stage of their civilizations, they don't pose a threat for humanity.

The aggressive image, you have of extraterrestrials, corresponds to your own nature – not to theirs.'

'I would sure love to see your planet,' Benedict sighed, 'but it is far too distant.'

'Would you like to travel a little through space with me?' Olep asked.

'Would that be possible?' Benedict asked back, excitedly.

'If you want to come along, look at me and concentrate on my center,' Olep offered.

Benedict gazed intensely at the orb. Suddenly, he had a feeling of being pulled into it. Through it, he saw the stars, and felt pulled upwards. He watched his house, his city, his country, the continent and Earth fall behind.

In next to no time, they were in space.

The Earth presented a sight to behold – far more magnificent even, than on the pictures from space that Benedict knew. His heart opened wide, as they floated through space. That indescribable beauty, that vastness and grandeur!

He was amazed at the wonders he perceived. Also, he heard fine harmonies, emanating from the planets and the stars.

'Oh,' Benedict whispered in awe, 'I didn't know, there was music in space.'

'Your poets knew of this music at all times, and called it "music of the spheres",' Olep remarked.

They traversed the solar system slowly, so that Benedict could admire the panorama at his leisure.

They came by Mars, and passed the asteroid belt between the inner and the outer planets.

The inner planets include Earth and Mars, Mercury and Venus, while the outer planets comprise the huge Jupiter, Saturn with its rings, Uranus and Neptune, which they also left behind.

In the distance, Benedict could see many thousands of other galaxies – it was ever so fascinating. This was, what he had always been dreaming of.

When they had left the solar system behind, they picked up speed. In the wink of an eye, they had reached the constellation Orion. Part of it was Rigel, a star system with several planets.

'This is my home planet,' Olep relayed.

Benedict only saw a desolate lump of rock.

'But life is not possible there, without water and atmosphere!' he stated disappointedly.

'And yet, there is life – it is just a little different from the way you know it,' Olep replied. 'Come and see.'

As they approached the surface, Benedict could make out beautiful buildings, as of crystal, with countless orbs like Olep floating in and out.

One of the buildings looked almost like a cathedral on Earth. It was of breathtaking beauty.

'What is that?' Benedict asked, amazed.

'That is something like a library, where you can access our entire knowledge. All you have to do, is think of a topic you are interested in, and all the information, we have on it, will be available to you,' Olep explained.

'Let us go there,' Benedict requested.

As they floated closer to the building, Benedict saw, that the space between the buildings shone with beautiful colors – colors, he had never seen on Earth. The surface was not at all desolate, but gorgeous.

Effortlessly, they penetrated the walls of the 'cathedral' – there were no doors. They were met by some of the orbs, who welcomed them warmly. Interested, they floated around Benedict to sense, where he came *from and who he was. All communication was word-less, with thought impressions.*

*Olep led Benedict to the main hall of the 'cathedral'.*

*'Ask your questions,' he invited him and Benedict didn't hesitate for a second. No sooner did he feel a question within him, than he received the answer, comprehensively, from every conceivable point of view.*

*He wanted to know, for example, what the natives of Olep's planet knew about Earth. The information he got was, of course, quite a surprise, because – need-less to say – they had quite a different perspective on all conditions there.*

*But he discovered, that his own knowledge and the attitudes of the other humans, were also part of the answers, which he received.*

*Of course, he also learned a lot about Olep's planet, its population and their way of life. He couldn't get enough of it.*

*'Why are you showing me all of this?' he asked Olep after a while.*

*Olep replied: 'Humanity is gradually evolving to-wards a new level of consciousness. We want to help speed up this process, because otherwise, irresponsi-ble humans will have destroyed Earth, before hu-mankind is fully developed.*

When the Earth-peoples have learned to interact more beneficially with each other and with their environment, they will also be ready for the contact with extraterrestrials, they desire so much. People like you can be pioneers and intermediaries in this regard.'

'But I am only a child!' Benedict exclaimed.

'That's exactly, why you're particularly suited for this purpose,' Olep commented. 'Your way of thinking is not yet as limited and fixed, as that of adult humans. You are still open to new impressions and concepts. This is a basic requirement for meeting other life forms.

You've seen enough for now. I'm going to take you back home again.'

'What a pity!' Benedict sighed. 'There is still so much to be explored and to inquire about.'

'We'll keep in touch,' Olep promised.

And as fast as they had reached Orion, they were back on Earth again. Happy and contented, Benedict sank into his bed and had a good night's sleep.

For the time being, he did not tell anyone about his journey, though, because no one, he knew of, would have understood him.

But Olep had told him, that he accompanied other humans in the same way, and so Benedict hoped, that *one day, he would meet people, to whom he could talk about extraterrestrials without being laughed at. Maybe you are one of them.*

# *Enchanted by the Light*

*There was once a lady named Liora, who brooded and mulled over, whatever happened to her. Every event, every word, every thought, she turned over in her mind and soul, heavily as a millstone. She made a problem out of everything that she experienced.*

*People, whom she was in contact with, felt sorry for her, because she was taking her life so hard, and they tried to direct her attention to the wonderful things that also existed in her life. But she did not let any ray of hope or suggestion for the improvement of her respective situation get to her.*

*So the people around her withdrew more and more, because it was very exhausting to turn over millstones with Liora, and it led nowhere.*

*Liora often grieved, because she felt forsaken, but she was far too busy with her millstones, to understand, that she had caused this herself. Thus she lived year in, year out, in the dark cave of her soul, without being able to find a way out.*

*One day, she saw a tiny point of light buzzing around her, and followed it with her eyes. After some time, she realized with surprise, that it was a living being - a firefly.*

*'Who are you?' Liora asked the firefly.*

'I am Raja – which means "Hope"!' it replied. 'The "Great Light" has sent me.'

'Light - what is that?' Liora inquired, amazed.

'I cannot explain that to you,' the firefly Raja answered, 'but come with me, I will show you!'

'Oh!' Liora sighed, 'I'm so tired. I cannot go with you!'

'May I at least come back tomorrow?' Raja requested.

'Well, all right,' Liora returned reluctantly, 'if it's not too long.'

Thus the firefly Raja came faithfully every day now, to see Liora – always asking permission beforehand, of course, because it did not want to impose itself on her.

After Liora had become accustomed to her dear visitor, it one day dared to ask:

'Would you mind, if I bring my friends along? Together it would be easier to give you an impression of, what light is like, than with one firefly alone.'

'Oh, I don't know,' Liora hesitated, 'so many at the same time might be too exhausting.'

But since she had come to trust Raja, she finally agreed.

The next day, a whole swarm of fireflies came into the dark cave and circled Liora. A glimmer of light illuminated the cave. Liora was overwhelmed and moved - it was so beautiful!

'So this is, what light looks like?' she asked shyly.

'That is just a pale reflection of the light you can find outside of your cave!' Raja replied. 'Come along with me!'

'Oh, I don't know,' Liora hesitated again, 'that might be dangerous – here, I know my way around.'

'So you would rather choose the known misfortune, than the unknown fortune?' the firefly probed.

But Liora did not change her mind.

'Then I would like you to meet a friend of mine. May I bring her with me tomorrow? You will like her,' Raja offered. Liora nodded her assent.

The next day brought a big surprise, for the firefly brought a kitten along, which was pushing a golden ball of wool in front of it. Liora was immediately taken in by the kitten, and even let it jump onto her lap, where she cuddled it tenderly. For the first time in ages, she felt a spark of love, and even joy, in her heart.

After some time, Raja suggested: 'Why don't you come out of the cave with us? All you have to do, is follow the golden thread that Yelina, the cat, brought with her.'

'Is there really anything outside of this cave?' Liora inquired. 'I've never been anywhere else, but here.'

'That's not true,' Raja objected. 'Remember: When you were younger – didn't you, time and again, experience moments of joy, even bliss, when you were completely absorbed in playing or roaming around in nature?'

Liora remembered. 'Are you suggesting, it could be like that again?' she questioned incredulously.

'It is never too late to start heading there. Come with us!' Raja beckoned.

Liora thought it over. The pleasant memory awakened a longing in her. She looked at the sweet kitten and the glowing fireflies, and finally she decided to give it a try. What did she have to lose?

The fireflies cheered and flew wild capers. Yelina, the cat, rubbed against Liora's legs, purring, and then returned to her ball of wool. Carefully, she pushed it back into the cave passage, which would lead them outside, and turned back to see, if Liora was following her.

It became a long walk – much longer, than it should have been, because Liora hesitated again and again, and turned back into the familiar darkness – then towards the light again, which she could see increase through the passage, and which was unfamiliar to her, but also attracted her.

Her companions, however, never lost patience, but persevered with her, enticing and encouraging her, until they finally reached the cave exit.

Words could not describe, what Liora's eyes beheld there. It made her so happy – even blissful – that she did not understand, why it had taken her so long, to find her way to the light.

'This is only the beginning!' Raja, the firefly, promised. 'But from here on, you will have to find your own path. We will leave you now. The "Great Light" will guide you and never leave you alone. Do not ever forget that! For there will still be ups and downs, but it need never be as dark again, as it has been for you.'

And although Liora could not imagine, that it would become even more beautiful, that is indeed, what happened. When she fully entrusted herself to the Light, she felt loved, safe and guided. When she doubted, the path became rockier, but she was never alone again, and the darkness was forever a thing of the past.

# The Return of the Unicorns

*Jason was raised by his grandmother. He didn't know, where his parents were, and he hardly ever asked himself, why he didn't live with his father and mother like the other children of the village.*

*His grandmother was a kind and wise woman, who lived with him in a small house at the edge of the woods. So he would often go into the forest, where he knew every bush and every tree. He loved to sit under a very old oak tree and savor the silence and the special atmosphere in the forest.*

*Early on, his grandmother taught him all about the healing effects of the herbs and fruits they found in the forest, and he was quick and eager to learn.*

*One day, he sat under the old oak tree again. The sun danced in the treetops. It was a beautiful day. Suddenly, he squinted his eyes, dazzled by an unexpected glare. When he opened them again, a white horse stood in front of him. It had a spiraled, long shining horn on its forehead. Jason felt awe at the sight of it, and sat there motionless.*

*The animal addressed him: 'Jason! A great task awaits you. You are needed in the Army of the Light.'*

*Jason was shocked: 'I am not suited for fighting!' he stammered. 'I am much too young and I am scared of war!'*

'This is no ordinary war,' the radiant being in front of him returned. 'It is a conflict between Light and Darkness, which, on the part of the Light, is only being fought with the weapons of love. You are a great healer. Are you willing to help us?'

'I don't know,' Jason stuttered. 'How could I be of help to you? I am not much of a healer, you know.'

'You are familiar with the healing effects of plants and will soon develop special healing powers yourself,' the being answered. 'The Warriors of the Darkness are fighting with all means for the retention of their power, leaving behind many injured in body and soul, who need your help.'

'I shall ask my grandmother,' Jason said hesitantly.

'Do so,' the being demanded. 'Talk to her, and if you wish, meet me here again tomorrow.'

His grandmother immediately sensed, that something extraordinary had happened, the moment Jason entered the house. But she waited patiently, until he began to talk of his own accord. Overwhelmed, he told her about his experience in the forest.

'A unicorn!' his grandmother whispered, awestruck, when he had finished. 'You are most blessed. Very few people have the privilege nowadays, of seeing such a being.'

'What is a unicorn?' Jason asked, puzzled.

In response, his grandmother began to narrate:

'Long, long ago, the world was full of unicorns. They are high spiritual beings, who made sure, that the world remained in balance and that all creatures had, what they needed.

As long as humans lived in peace with each other, and in harmony with nature, they could even perceive these delicate and shy beings. But as the world grew louder, and people increasingly sought only their own advantage, this gift was lost. Little by little, the unicorns then disappeared from the face of the Earth.

But now, that the darkness is becoming ever darker, and the light ever lighter, they have been returning, to assist the Army of the Light against the Dark Forces. When they encounter human beings of pure heart, they touch them with their shining horns, so that their hearts become strong with love, which will make them invulnerable. Thus empowered, such humans join the other Forces of the Light, and they drive back the Darkness in the world.'

'How do you know that?' Jason asked her, amazed.

'You can find all this in ancient records,' his grandmother smiled. 'It's just, that they are taken for fairy tales by most people.'

'What should I do now?' Jason inquired.

'Follow your heart!' she advised him. 'You better sleep on it. Tomorrow you can make your decision.'

During the night, Jason had a dream: He was wandering through a dark valley, when suddenly a sunbeam broke through the clouds and bathed everything in a golden light. The world was transformed.

And he heard a voice: 'Fear not! Light is always stronger than darkness. Love will prevail!'

Thus, in the morning, he decided to go back into the forest to see the unicorn again. He sat down under the old oak and waited. Suddenly, he felt a breath of air, and when he looked up, the unicorn stood in front of him again.

'Well?' it inquired. 'What is your decision?'

Jason stood up. 'I would love to help you, but I don't want to leave my grandmother alone.'

'You need not leave your home, for the time being,' the unicorn said. 'You shall fulfill your duties, wherever you are, on the people that are led into your path.'

'I see!' Jason exclaimed, relieved. 'Then I am ready for it.'

'Jason – Healer!' the unicorn addressed him, 'Kneel down! Receive the armor of the Light: The Love that can heal body and soul, the Spirit of Truth and the wisdom to discern the good and evil powers of the spiritual world. You may rise – you are now part of the Army of the Light!'

Having said this, the unicorn touched Jason with its

*shining horn, and he felt love, peace and joy flowing into his heart, and all of his fear vanishing.*

*What happens next?' Jason asked the unicorn.*

*It replied: 'Return home now. Learn as much as you can, show love and appreciation to any being you meet. Everything else will come about at the proper time.*

*Jason bowed to the unicorn and headed for home. When he had almost reached the house, the neighbor's cat came towards him. It was limping and meowing miserably. Jason bent down and saw, that it had a thorn in its paw. He pulled the thorn out, and held the paw gently in his hands. Suddenly, he felt warmth emanating from his hands. The wound immediately stopped bleeding.*

*Jason had never experienced anything like it. The cat rubbed against his leg, purring gratefully. Deep in thought, Jason returned home.*

*Some other time, when he was out in the village again, he saw a child fall, while trying to climb over a wall, and start crying. Jason took the child up in his arms and then put his hand on the child's bleeding knee. Again, warmth emanated from his hand. The child calmed down and the wound began to heal.*

*Its mother, who had come running from the house, when she heard her child cry, saw the miracle and was awed.*

'My mother is sick in bed and in pain. Could you help her, too, maybe?' she asked full of hope.

'I can try,' Jason answered shyly and followed her into the house.

The old lady was delighted with the unexpected visitor, and Jason asked her, where it hurt, and if he might touch her. Then he carefully laid his hand on her head and on the painful spot. Immediately, she felt better, and smiled gratefully at him.

Word of Jason's gift soon spread, and from all over the village, sick people soon came to his grandmother's house or he was called to theirs. Either they prepared herbs to help the sick, or Jason laid his hands on them. Most of them returned home, strengthened and healed. But he could not help all of them.

Once, when he entered the house of a sick person, he immediately sensed the tense, uneasy atmosphere between her and the relatives, who had summoned him. In the eyes of the sick person, he saw only hatred and resentment.

She received him with venomous words. When he asked her permission to touch her, she insulted him.

Puzzled, he asked her: 'What is it, you want me to do for you?'

She answered: 'If you cannot see that for yourself, you are incompetent. Then you can leave right away!'

Downcast, Jason left the house, without having achieved anything.

Back home, he asked his grandmother: 'Why couldn't I heal this person?'

His grandmother answered: 'The healing energies only flow, if someone is ready to receive them. A person, who allows too much space for darkness, is no longer open to the healing power of the Light.'

Jason enjoyed helping people and did his work humbly and patiently. With the gifts of gratitude from their patients, he provided for himself and his grandmother, who was gradually becoming frail.

One morning, Jason's grandmother called him to her bedside: 'The time has come for me to die. You have found your path. Follow it faithfully in love and truth. Then you will want for nothing all your life.'

'No, dear grandmother, you must not go. I will heal you!' Jason cried, distraught.

His grandmother smiled weakly: 'Death is not a disease. It cannot be healed. It is only the gateway to the world, from which we came, before we entered the Earth. Don't cry. I will always be around you. But it is now time to tell you the truth about your parents:

Years ago – not long after you were born – the Ruler of the Pointed Black Rock, from the neighboring country, attacked our people. Your parents were healers, as well – just like you, and wanted to assist the Army of the Light, which our ruler also served, with their gifts. They left for the neighboring country and never returned.'

'Why did they leave?' Jason asked, agitated.

'They were trying to help you and everyone else in this country survive. The Ruler of the Pointed Black Rock had covered this land with parasites, which threatened to destroy all harvests. The people were starving, and only the brave actions of the Army of the Light could drive the locusts back.'

'What happened to my parents, then?' Jason asked, distressed.

'This is something, only you can find out. The unicorns will help you.'

With these words, his grandmother closed her eyes and passed away.

Jason was beside himself with pain and grief. Desperate, he fled into the forest to clear his mind. He hoped to meet the unicorn again there. But it did not come.

A few days after his grandmother's funeral, people began to approach him again about helping their sick. But Jason quickly realized, that his hands had lost their healing touch. He didn't know, what to make of it.

No sooner had the villagers noticed this, than they began to insult him: 'Now that your grandmother, the old witch, does not help you anymore with her magic, you cannot accomplish anything.'

Jason felt humiliated and furious. Without further ado, he packed up a few belongings, took his bag of herbs, and left the village to search for his parents.

He wandered through many villages and towns. Everywhere he offered his help. He healed the sick with the herbs he collected on the way – his own healing powers had left him, after all. For his services, he was given food and sometimes even quarters for the night.

Time and again, he inquired about the 'Ruler of the Pointed Black Rock', his grandmother had told him about, but no one had ever heard of him.

Gradually, Jason noticed, that the land was becoming more and more barren. The soil was poor and the people looked emaciated.

One night – it was already late – he came to a small house and knocked on the door. An elderly woman opened.

'What do you want?' she asked grumpily.

He offered her his help and asked for quarters and something to eat, since he couldn't continue his journey because of the darkness.

'We have nothing to eat for ourselves!' the woman snarled at him. She was about to send him away, when a sweet voice sounded from the background: 'Let him in, Martha!'

Reluctantly, the woman admitted him into the house. When he entered, he saw a girl sitting in the living room, who looked at him with friendly, clear eyes.

'I am not sure, that this is a good idea!' Martha made herself heard, but the girl stopped her with a wave of her hand and welcomed Jason warmly.

'Bring something to eat and prepare a place to sleep for our guest,' she instructed Martha, who retreated to comply, grumbling under her breath.

'My name is Daria,' the girl introduced herself. 'Who are you, and what are you doing here?'

'I'm Jason,' he answered. 'I am searching for my parents, who have been missing.'

'What happened?' Daria asked compassionately.

'My grandmother, who raised me, mentioned a 'Ruler of the Pointed Black Rock', who they fought against, to save our country. But they never returned, and no one I met on all my journeys, knew of this ruler,' Jason confided to her.

'I know him well,' Daria said softly, lowering her head. 'He caused my parents' deaths, as well.

And it is because of him, that I can't move my legs anymore, and that I am confined to the house.'

Only then, did Jason notice, that her legs were crippled. Sad, he replied: 'Before my grandmother died, I could heal people with my hands, but unfortunately I have lost this gift or I would help you.'

'Oh, are you also part of the Army of the Light?' Daria asked, surprised.

'You know about it?' Jason asked back excitedly.

'Yes!' she replied, 'The unicorns have told me about it.'

'You can see unicorns?' Jason marveled. 'It has been quite some time, since I have seen one, although I thought, they would always be around,' he added despondently.

'Could it be, that you have been sad or furious a lot, lately?' Daria asked cautiously. Jason confirmed it.

'Then you cannot see them, for unicorns can only be perceived by people, who are at peace with themselves. This may also be the reason, why you can't heal people anymore,' Daria pointed out. 'You have to forgive everybody, who has hurt you, so that peace will return to your heart and you can heal.'

'I can't!' Jason exclaimed.

'Try! Even if it takes a while,' Daria asked of him, pleadingly. 'Forgiveness is often a lengthy process, but you have to consciously choose it.'

At that moment, Martha entered with his dinner. She couldn't offer him more than dry bread and some water. After the meager meal, they all retired.

Breakfast was as meager as dinner. When Jason asked, why the land was so barren, Daria sighed and answered:

'I feel, the Ruler of the Pointed Black Rock is responsible for this, but I cannot prove it, and no one believes me. He is cutting off our water, so that nothing can grow anymore.'

'How long has this been going on?' Jason inquired.

'It has been a gradual, insidious development. We did not notice it, until it was too late,' Daria explained. 'And we are not the only ones, this is happening to.'

'Something's got to be done!' Jason shouted. 'I have to find him!'

'Do you want to take revenge, or do you want to help us?' Daria asked, looking at him.

Jason hesitated for a moment, and then replied:

'I want to stop the scheming of this ruler, because he spreads darkness and people cannot defend themselves against him. I promised to serve the Army of the Light!'

Thus, Daria took a silver chain with a compass that she had worn around her neck, put it on Jason's neck and said:

'This compass is a gift to you from the unicorns. All you have to do, is tell it, where you want to go, and it will show you the way.'

'If I only knew, how to cope with this ruler!' Jason brooded.

'You have to find the Magic Penny, which empowers him, and destroy it,' Daria answered. 'The unicorns have told me, that he cannot do anything without the magic of this Penny. Good luck!'

So Jason set off again. 'To the Pointed Black Rock!' he instructed the compass, and instantly the needle pointed into the right direction.

After several days' journey, he caught sight of a pointed Pointed Black Rock in the distance. When he got closer, he saw, that a fortress had been carved into the rock. It was surrounded by a vast and deep water moat. Jason tried to find a way to cross the moat, without being detected, because he could see guards patrolling the battlements of the fortress.

He waited for nightfall, and selected a secluded spot to get into the water. The water was bitter cold. It virtually took his breath away. He left his bag of herbs and his bundle behind, on the edge of the moat, and bravely started swimming, trying to make as little noise as possible.

Every now and then, Jason looked up at the fortress. The closer he came to the rock, the more a strange anxiety and trepidation took hold of him, as if the Darkness wanted to take possession of his soul. He thought of the unicorns and he thought of Daria. This gave him the strength to keep on swimming.

The moat was very, very wide, but eventually Jason reached the rock undetected and climbed ashore. He discovered a window, squeezed through, and found himself in a dark chamber. Jason tried to feel his surroundings.

The chamber was damp and seemed to contain all sorts of junk. Several times, he bumped into objects in the dark and hurt himself. At last, he found a door. He listened attentively for sounds from outside, but everything was quiet. So he ventured out into the hallway.

'Find the Penny!' he whispered to the compass, and the needle complied, indicating the direction.

Suddenly, Jason heard footsteps. He quickly hid in an alcove. Frightened, he held his breath, but the guards patrolling by, did not see him. Relieved, he continued on his way, after a while.

The Ruler of the Pointed Black Rock slept fitfully that night. After some time, he called his servant and said to him:

'Something is different tonight. I feel, that Light has entered the fortress. Have everything searched!'

Thus, all available guards and soldiers soon swarmed through the fortress. Jason hardly made any progress, because he had to hide time and time again. But his compass finally led him through a secret passage and, before he knew it, he was standing in the throne room. On a pedestal, he saw the Magic Penny. But no sooner had he touched it, than the doors burst open and the Ruler's soldiers rushed in.

'Get him!' one of them shouted. Jason backed off. 'He has got the Penny!' another shouted.

Then the Ruler himself entered. Everyone in the room froze. When his gaze met Jason's, Jason felt fear and horror gripping him. His limbs became heavy as lead. His despair gave him the strength, however, to break the spell and throw the Penny out of the window.

The soldiers closed in on him, with their weapons raised. They had surrounded him, and some pointed their weapons at him, to put an end to his life.

Suddenly, a terrible rumbling sounded, and the ground began to tremble. Everyone tried to keep on their feet somehow. The whole rock was shaking. Stones began to crumble from the ceiling and the walls. Jason sank to the ground, hit by a stone.

When he regained consciousness, he was lying outdoors and saw a unicorn above him. It touched him with its shining horn. Immediately he felt strengthened and was able to stand up again.

He recognized the unicorn that had healed him, as the one that had spoken to him in the forest.

'What happened?' he asked it, confused. He was surrounded by unicorns.

His unicorn spoke to him: 'You did a good job! When the Magic Penny fell into the water moat, it lost its magic properties, so that the Army of the Light gained access to the fortress. It is now destroyed, and the power of the clandestine ruler of the world is shattered. Unfortunately, he himself has escaped, but he will never be able to re-establish that much power again – now that the unicorns have returned to Earth.'

'What about my parents?' Jason asked the unicorn.

'They are not on the Earth-plane anymore,' it replied, 'but we have found someone else, who loves you and is waiting for you. Turn around!'

When Jason turned around, he saw Daria sitting on a unicorn. She stretched her arms out to him, and he caught her, as she slid off the unicorn's back. They hugged affectionately.

'Dear Jason, dear Daria!' the unicorn spoke, 'You have faithfully served the Army of the Light and have acquired sufficient love and wisdom, to be able to rule over your country. Are you willing to?'

*They looked at each other and then at the unicorn. Their eyes said it all.*

*'Receive our blessing then, and pass it on to anyone you meet!' the unicorn said to them. Then it touched Daria's crippled legs with its horn. Instantly, they were healed and Daria jumped with joy.*

*The unicorns took the two to the castle of the ruler, with whom Jason's parents had set out in their day in the service of the Light, for he, too, had not returned.*

*There they lived long and in peace and ruled wisely.*

# The Melancholic Butterfly

*Once upon a time, there was a little colorful butterfly. She was sitting on a flower, as she often did, and sighing deeply, even sucking the most delicious nectar.*

*'What are you sighing so deeply for?' a bee, buzzing by, asked her.*

*'Oh!' the little butterfly moaned, 'Life is so dreadfully tough!'*

*'What makes it so tough for you?' the bee asked, surprised.*

*'Well,' the butterfly replied, 'it is so exhausting to flutter from flower to flower, to gather sufficient food.'*

*Puzzled, the bee returned: 'Why is that? You only have to take care of yourself! Look at me! I have to provide for a whole swarm of bees, and yet I'm always cheerful at work, humming a little song to myself. Take it easy! You are a butterfly, after all!'*

*And off she went.*

*The little butterfly thought about it.*

*But soon, she lowered her proboscis into the next flower with a sigh. An earthworm poked his head out of the ground: 'What are you sighing so deeply for?'*

*'Oh!' the butterfly answered, 'It is a constant struggle to gather sufficient food for myself.'*

'Be happy, that you can fly!' the earthworm objected. 'When you were still a caterpillar, you had to crawl on the ground like me.

But you have grown wings, while I must continue toiling through the soil, and yet, I always have everything I need in abundance. For that I am very grateful. Maybe you make it too hard for yourself. Keep your mind on the good things in your life!'

The little butterfly thought about it.

It didn't take long, however, and she fluttered on to the next flower, sighing. A bumblebee overheard it, and asked sympathetically: 'What are you sighing so deeply for?'

'Oh!' the butterfly replied, 'It is so hard to fight the wind, when I fly from one flower to the next. It costs me so much energy!'

The bumblebee responded: 'I understand that. Look at me! My body is actually too heavy for my little wings, but I let the wind carry me, instead of fighting it.'

'But then I won't get to the exact flower, I want to get to,' the butterfly returned.

'Well, you don't know, if the wind would not carry you to an even more delicious flower, do you?' the wise bumblebee pointed out. 'You cannot defeat the wind, but you can make him your friend.

*Don't take yourself too seriously, and allow yourself to be guided. Just try it!'*

*The little butterfly did. When the wind blew in her face, she henceforth turned around and let herself be carried by the breeze. And she realized, that she never suffered want, even then.*

*For the first time in her life, she felt light as a butterfly.*

# How Scaredy-Cat Became Lionheart

*Once upon a time, there was a little girl. Everyone just called her "Scaredy-Cat", because she was scared of everything and everybody. She was scared of her playfellows: scared, they wouldn't like her, they would hurt her or they would make fun of her. She was scared of animals, they would frighten or even bite her.*

*She was scared of thunderstorms. She was scared of ghosts and scared of witches. She was scared to stand out and scared to stand up for herself, scared to hurt herself, scared to hurt others – in a nutshell: Her life was full of fears, that kept her from cheerfully and joyfully walking her path.*

*Every time she got scared – which was quite often – she fled into her bed, for there it was warm and she felt safe and secure. People just shook their heads at Scaredy-Cat. Some even laughed at her.*

*One night, when Scaredy-Cat was lying in bed with the blanket pulled over her head, because a mighty storm was raging outside, she heard someone calling softly. It sounded so sweet and bell-like – very close-by. A gentle voice called her name.*

*Scaredy-Cat was never ever called by her real name! Surprised, she peeked out from under her blanket. At first, she couldn't recognize anything. But then, she saw a graceful little being, with fine transparent* wings, sitting on the window sill. Scaredy-Cat lived up to her name, and promptly got scared.

'Don't be afraid!' the delicate being encouraged her.

'Who are you?' Scaredy-Cat dared to ask.

'I am the fairy Lumia,' the being on the window sill said. 'You need not be scared – I want to be your friend.'

Scaredy-Cat was amazed: 'There really are fairies! I have always wanted to meet one.'

Scaredy-Cat pulled the blanket off her head, and took a closer look at the fairy. She had a beautiful, sweet face, and so Scaredy-Cat set aside her fear, little by little.

'Where do you come from? What are you doing here?' she asked the fairy.

'I have come to play with you,' she replied.

'With me?' Scaredy-Cat asked timidly, 'You want to play with me, of all people?'

'Of course!' the fairy exclaimed cheerfully. 'Let us start right away!'

So they played with each other all night. Scaredy-Cat was happy. Of course, she had initially been scared, she might damage the delicate little creature, but then they were so absorbed in their play that she forgot about this fear.

At daybreak, Lumia said goodbye and disappeared. Scaredy-Cat rubbed her eyes. Had all this only been a dream or had she really played with a fairy?

When her mother entered the room to wake her up, Scaredy-Cat was still filled with her experience and her words came out all in a tumble, when she tried to tell her mother about it.

'Nonsense!' her mother scolded her. 'You were just dreaming. Come on and get ready!'

Disappointed, Scaredy-Cat decided to keep her experience to herself from now on, for it was precious to her. It was difficult for her, though. She was so excited, and didn't want to let it show. Hardly could she await the next night.

And indeed: No sooner did Scaredy-Cat lie in bed and it became quiet outside, than she heard somebody call her name again. Very cautiously she peered at the window sill and there she was: Lumia, smiling at her.

'You are real, aren't you?' Scaredy-Cat asked.

Lumia laughed her bell-like laughter: 'Let us play and you shall see!'

So they played with each other again, all night. Scaredy-Cat was happy. This went on many a night. By night Scaredy-Cat played, by day she was scared.

One night Lumia said: 'I want to take you on a trip.' 'Oh, no!' Scaredy-Cat cried. 'Let us stay here. I'm scared!'

'It is not far,' Lumia replied. 'Come with me, I'll show you something.'

She took her to the other end of the room, where Scaredy-Cat found herself standing in front of a large mirror.

'Take a look. What do you see?' Lumia asked her.

Scaredy-Cat stared into the mirror. Therein, she saw a beautiful princess, gorgeously dressed, looking out at her.

'Who is she?' Scaredy-Cat whispered, fascinated.

'This is the Princess Lionheart!' Lumia answered. 'Would you like to meet her?'

'Oh, yes!' Scaredy-Cat exclaimed, and forgot to be scared.

'Close your eyes and hold my hand,' the fairy instructed her. Trustingly, Scaredy-Cat closed her eyes. Lumia took her hand and continued:

'Now take three steps forward. But you must not open your eyes!'

Scaredy-Cat obeyed. Suddenly, she felt soft ground under her feet and a gentle breeze on her cheek. Startled, she opened her eyes: She was standing in the middle of a forest.

'Where are we?' Scaredy-Cat asked, with a start. But Lumia had disappeared. The sun was shining through the trees and the birds were singing. Scaredy-Cat looked around. Nearby, two squirrels were chasing each other up a tree. A rabbit lolloped by.

She took a few tentative steps, and reached a clearing, from where she could see a beautiful golden castle. Fascinated, she walked towards it. When she approached the gate, the gate-keeper stood open-mouthed with amazement.

'Princess Lionheart!' he exclaimed in disbelief.

'No, it is just me – Scaredy-Cat,' she said timidly.

But the gate-keeper turned around, and ran into the courtyard of the castle, shouting: 'Our Princess Lionheart is back!'

There was great excitement, hustle and bustle. Finally, a little boy came up to the gate, full of curiosity: 'Hello, my Princess, won't you come in?'

Scaredy-Cat was scared. 'I think, you are mistaking me for someone else,' she whispered shyly.

But a delegation of courtiers already came out of the gate and greeted her warmly. 'Thank God!' they exclaimed, 'The Princess is back.'

Scaredy-Cat wanted to object, but nobody heeded her. They bowed respectfully before her and led her into the castle courtyard.

Thence, they were met by the Imperial Chancellor Justin, who was in charge of the state affairs and wanted to find out the reason for the disturbance in the court-yard.

'Princess Lionheart!' he, too, exclaimed, hardly believing his eyes. Overjoyed, he greeted her: 'You are back from your journey at last! How good to see you!'

More and more people came to welcome the Princess. All were beside themselves with amazement and joy. Scaredy-Cat didn't understand, what was happening to her. Several times, she tried to clear up the misunderstanding, but nobody listened to her. Soon she began to have doubts herself.

'Benjamin!' – The name escaped her lips, when the little boy from the gate jumped cheerfully towards her.

'Oh, you are beginning to remember!' he rejoiced and hugged his princess.

In the courtyard, the stable boy came to meet her with a beautiful white pony.

'Cherry-Blossom!' she said, lost in thought. The pony pressed against her arm with affection. Somehow, it seemed familiar to her.

Little by little, more details came back to her. The longer she stayed in the castle, the more natural it felt to her. Everyone seemed happy to see her.

'But how come, you all know me? I have never been here before!' she wondered.

*Justin, the Imperial Chancellor, smiled at her and answered: 'Dear Princess, you have been absent for a long time and have now returned. Rest now from the stresses and strains of your journey and feel at home with us again.'*

*Saying this, he accompanied her to her chambers and showed her, where she could rest. Gratefully, the Princess dropped onto the bed, when she was alone at last, and was soon sound asleep.*

*In the castle, however, the excitement continued. There was a lot to do, now that the Princess was back. Even though her belongings had always been kept ready for her, everything was brightly polished now, her clothing put in order, her friends notified, her animals fetched, and a great banquet prepared.*

*When the Princess woke up, a friend was already standing by, to help her change her clothes.*

*'Patricia,' the Princess remembered.*

*'Welcome home!' Patricia smiled. 'You have been gone for quite a long time.'*

*'I don't understand all this,' the Princess stammered. 'Why am I suddenly a princess? Why have I been gone? Where have I been?'*

*'You have always been a princess. You just forgot. You were far, far away,' Patricia explained to her. 'There will be a great banquet in your honor. Come!'*

It was a grand celebration. Many people, who were important to the Princess, came, and they enjoyed a happy reunion. The festivities lasted for three days. The animals were cared for, just like all the other guests, and everybody had a good time.

Everyone at the court was eager to fulfill the Princess her every wish. With her recently regained friends, she went for long horse rides. She rode Cherry-Blossom, her beloved pony.

She and her friends often played with each other, swam in the nearby river, had long intense conversations on this, that and everything, and enjoyed their time together.

But there was also work to do for the Princess.

Justin, the Imperial Chancellor, introduced her to the state affairs, and with her friends, she began to care for the needs of the inhabitants of her kingdom.

Nobody lacked anything. Everyone was allowed to say, what they needed, without fear, and thus had enough and to spare.

The Princess herself, felt better and better. Under the love of those around her, she blossomed and gained new self-confidence. Soon she forgot about her life as Scaredy-Cat. Nobody in her kingdom knew of it anyway. Everyone treated her, as it befitted her dignity as a princess.

Every day, she performed her duties with pleasure, and there was always spare-time enough, to be with the people she loved. There was no reason to lose heart anymore. So she became lion-hearted again.

Sometime later, Princess Lionheart went swimming in the river with her friends again. They splashed and teased each other, and had a lot of fun.

'Let us have a swimming contest!' the Princess shouted playfully. Everyone was thrilled.

The Princess swam to the other bank, as fast as she could, leaving the others far behind.

When she got out of the water, her mother suddenly stood in front of her and exclaimed:

'Scaredy-Cat! Where on earth have you been? We have been searching for you all over the place!'

'I am Lionheart!' the Princess returned self-confident-ly. 'And I have been home.'

Her mother looked at her blankly.

'Well, all that matters is, that you are back and nothing happened to you,' she finally replied.

'On the contrary! A lot has happened!' Lionheart smiled.

Everyone was amazed at her, and at how much she had changed, and nobody dared to call her "Scaredy-Cat" anymore.

From now on she was called "Lionheart".

# The Little Sunbeam's Adventures

There was once an inquisitive little sunbeam. On his first visit to Earth with the others, they landed on a colorful flower meadow. Cheeky, as he was, he kissed the first flower he met, on her closed bloom. She awoke and opened her petals.

'Good morning, dear sun,' she greeted him, 'I thank you.'

'What for?' the little sunbeam asked her.

'Your light means life and nourishment for me,' the flower replied.

'Oh, I'm delighted!' the little sunbeam exclaimed and beamed.

A little later, he came to a small house. He peeked through the window. Inside sat an old lady, knitting. She seemed to be very sad. When she caught sight of the little sunbeam, her face lit up.

'Come in, dear sun,' she invited him. He didn't need to be told twice.

'What are you doing here, and why are you so sad?' he asked the lady.

'I cannot pay my electricity bill,' she answered. 'So I am sitting here in the dark, knitting, trying to earn some money. But wherever you are present, it is getting brighter and the darkness has to withdraw.'

'Darkness, what is that?' the little sunbeam wanted to know.

'Darkness is not really anything. It is more like nothing – basically, it is just the absence of light. Light is something – darkness is not,' the lady tried to explain.

'If darkness is nothing, why does it make you sad?' the little sunbeam inquired.

'Darkness makes the heart feel empty and burdened. And when you feel burdened, you feel sad,' the lady replied. 'But you even overcome the sadness. I am so glad you are here! For where there is light, darkness cannot persist.'

'Well, that's most interesting!' the little sunbeam commented. 'I would sure like to see the darkness sometime.'

'You can't – your light disperses it. Darkness has no effect on light. Light, however, annihilates darkness,' the lady returned.

'That's, how strong I am!' the little sunbeam rejoiced.

'Yes, you are indeed,' the lady confirmed. 'I thank you. Now my heart feels lighter again.' Deep in thought, the little sunbeam left the house.

There was a cat lying on the little wall in front of the house. He began to purr, when the little sunbeam stroked his fur, and stretched luxuriously.

'Do you know the darkness?' the little sunbeam asked him.

'Of course! Darkness is, when your prey cannot see you. This means easy hunting and always a good meal,' the cat answered, licking his mouth.

'I see,' the little sunbeam muttered, somewhat at a loss, and moved on.

Through the window of the next house, he could see into a room, wherein an old man was lying sick in his bed. When he spotted the little sunbeam, he yelled: 'Get out of here at once! I don't want to be bothered!' Alarmed, his daughter rushed in.

'Close those shutters immediately!' the old man screamed at her. His daughter hurried to comply in such a haste, that she almost pinched the little sunbeam.

'Well, what was this all about?' he thought to himself. 'All others have always been happy to see me! I wonder, if this is what darkness looks like.'

'Dance with me!' a soft voice above him interrupted his thoughts. Up there, a colorful butterfly fluttered back and forth between the twigs of a tree. The little sunbeam was only too happy to be distracted. They danced around each other between the leaves, until the butterfly had to rest exhaustedly on a flower.

'What is darkness?' the little sunbeam wanted to know from the butterfly.

'Darkness is, when you sleep snugly in your cocoon, before you see the light of day as a butterfly,' it answered and fluttered away.

'So darkness can also be something nice!' the little sunbeam mused.

In the marketplace, he encountered a beggar, who had fallen asleep in front of a store, with a hat full of coins in front of him. The little sunbeam tickled his nose. So the beggar woke up and looked around to see, what had disturbed him.

'Do you know, what darkness is?' the little sunbeam asked him.

'Of course!' the beggar answered. 'Darkness is, when you have lost hope, that things will get any better – like walking through a long tunnel and seeing no light at its end.'

'Oh,' the little sunbeam mumbled sympathetically, 'there's got to be something, one can do about it!'

'Maybe,' the beggar reflected, 'we just have to pay more attention to the light that is present – like you, for example, just now. And ultimately, any tunnel will end.'

'Isn't there anything positive about darkness?' the little sunbeam inquired.

The beggar thought about it: 'Darkness also means shelter and silence, to be allowed to retire and rest unobserved, forgetting one's worries for a while.'

It was already afternoon, and the little sunbeam found a beautiful garden, where two friends were sitting at a table, chatting. He danced on the table and in their glasses, which they were absolutely delighted about.

'What is darkness?' the little sunbeam finally wanted to know from them, as well.

'Darkness is the absence of love,' one of them said.

'Or the presence of conflicts and misunderstandings,' the other added.

'So is love also something like light?' he inquired.

'Yes!' the answer came. 'Something like light for the heart!'

'Well, then it's all very simple!' the little sunbeam exclaimed, overjoyed. 'The sun just needs to shine into every heart, and all darkness within will be gone in an instant!'

'Love, unlike sunlight, can only be passed from heart to heart,' one of the friends pointed out. 'The sun can, unfortunately, not do this for us.'

'But when the sun is shining,' the other commented, 'people feel better and spread more love – so you have a point there.'

'I want so much to help make everyone feel better!' the little sunbeam sighed.

'You have been doing that all along! We are very grateful to you,' the two friends replied. Comforted, the little sunbeam left them.

At dusk, he returned to the flower meadow, where he had landed in the morning.

'Good night!' the flower, he had kissed awake in the morning, called out to him. 'I am looking forward to seeing you again tomorrow.'

The little sunbeam blushed and hid behind a cloud. Shortly thereafter, he returned home with all his siblings, tired but content.

'This has been an exciting first day on Earth,' he thought to himself, looking forward to the next day. Soon he was sound asleep. He experienced many, many more adventures, but he never got to know the darkness.

# The Invisible Princess

*There was once a little princess, whose name was Sophia. She was always cheerful and friendly and everybody in the castle just loved her. Like all other royal children, she didn't go to school, of course, but had her own tutors, who had to teach no one but her.*

*Ms. Woodpecker, who was also responsible for the library, taught her everything about the deeds and misdeeds of great rulers, the works of great poets and the pictures of great artists. She was very strict, wore her hair in a bun, and had thick glasses, through which her eyes looked small and almost a bit wicked. She attached great importance to timeliness and watched like a hawk, whether the princess was properly dressed and had clean fingernails.*

*Furthermore, there was Mr. Joy. He was an elderly gentleman with white hair and many laugh-lines in his face. His clear blue eyes always shone with a pleasant warmth and kindliness, which made the princess feel immediately at ease. Mr. Joy was the princess' best friend and closest confidant. He taught her everything about the plants and the animals in the large park that surrounded the castle, about the wind and the clouds, about the stars and the universe, and about God.*

*When the weather was nice, his lessons were usually given in the park – not the library – where he taught*

Sophia to observe the characteristics and needs of the various plants and animals and to forecast the weather by watching the clouds.

He seemed to know all the answers. And if he couldn't think of an answer shortly, he wouldn't, like the other grown-ups, say: 'You are too young to understand that'. But he would say: 'Let me think about it for a moment.' Then Sophia had to be quiet as a mouse, while he laid a finger at his nose and stared into the air. After some time of reflection, he could usually answer Sophia's question. Otherwise he would simply admit:

'I don't know.'

The princess was an eager student. Since the lessons of Ms. Woodpecker didn't interest her, she simply memorized everything, for Ms. Woodpecker examined her frequently, and was not satisfied, unless Sophia could reproduce all names and data accurately.

After she had fulfilled these bothersome obligations, she went overjoyed into the park to observe the animals and play with them, whereby she learned a lot. She told Mr. Joy about it, and asked him, what she didn't understand.

He explained everything to her, and made her explain it back to him to see, if she had understood it all. If not, he didn't put the blame on her, like Ms. Woodpecker did, but on himself, because he had not explained it well enough in the first place.

Thus, the little princess grew up gaining in beauty and wisdom. She didn't have to worry about anything, always having plenty of food, nice clothing, toys as many as she wished, and being loved by everyone around.

When the princess turned twelve years of age, however, something happened, that changed her life:

People began to overlook her! As usual, she greeted everyone she met in her friendly manner, but more and more frequently, people passed her by without returning her greeting, as if they hadn't noticed her. At first, this only happened in the evenings, when it was already dark, in the long corridors of the castle, which were poorly lit, so that the princess thought:

'They are probably tired and didn't see me in the dark.' But increasingly, people soon passed her even in bright daylight, without perceiving her.

The princess became increasingly sad, indeed, when she greeted people in her friendly way, and they did not take notice of her. Even her parents didn't turn around anymore, when she entered the room.

One day, she actually heard them complain, that they hardly got to see their daughter anymore, while Sophia was, in fact, standing in the room! Bewildered, she shouted: 'I am here. Why do you keep ignoring me?' But her voice sounded like the whispering of the wind, and her parents didn't hear her.

Sophia was appalled, but there was no time to think about it, for she had to hurry, if she wanted to be on time for Ms. Woodpecker's lessons. Breathlessly, she arrived in the library and sat down on her seat opposite of Ms. Woodpecker. She ignored Sophia and looked at the door instead, checked the clock, looked at the door again, and grumbled:

'Why can't this brat ever be on time?'

Sophia said: 'I am here!' Ms. Woodpecker didn't react. Sophia became frightened. She waved her arms in front of Ms. Woodpecker's face and shouted:

'Hello, here I am!'

Ms. Woodpecker only heard a whisper as of the wind and felt a slight breeze. 'Well,' she mumbled, 'somebody must have forgotten again to close the window.'

Horror and fright seized Sophia. 'Ms. Woodpecker! Ms. Woodpecker!' she screamed. But the latter didn't hear her, and apparently she couldn't see her either!

Sophia hurried away from the library and rushed into the park. She was utterly confused and desperate.

In the park, she came across her cat Philo, who rubbed against her legs, purring. 'You see me!' Sophia exclaimed, surprised, and was consoled a bit. 'What's wrong with all those people?' By and by, her other animal-friends came to her, and they played with each other.

In the afternoon, Mr. Joy came into the park for their lessons and greeted her kindly. Sobbing and relieved she threw herself into his arms and told him about her strange experiences. 'It seems to me, that people cannot see me. How come, you can?'

Mr. Joy thought about it. After a while he answered carefully:

'You know, there are people, who can perceive with their hearts, as children do. Most grown-ups, however, cannot really see anymore, and we become invisible to them, when we grow up ourselves, just as they become invisible to us with time. Then we are left to see only the masks that we show to each other.

'But I cannot live like that!' Sophia sobbed, 'Not to be seen anymore! Is there no other way?'

'Yes, there is,' Mr. Joy comforted her. 'There is a land, where everybody perceives with their hearts. If you want to remain true to yourself, you have to go searching for it. That is the meaning of life.

On your way there, you have to pass many a test, but when you will have found the Land of the Perceptive Hearts, you will there be given the Golden Cloak. Whoever wears it, can again perceive the person behind the mask and be seen herself.'

'But how will I find the way there?' Sophia wanted to know.

'The way can only be found by walking it. You never see more than the next step,' came the answer. 'You better start right away. Don't take anything along. Everything you need, will be supplied, when you need it.'

Thus Sophia said goodbye to Mr. Joy and her animals and left the court without a moment's hesitation. She bid farewell to no one else, since they could not see her anymore!

After a short walk, she reached the big city, near which the castle was situated. There she saw many beggars sitting in the streets. She felt sorry for them and tried to get into contact with them. But the beggars didn't see her, either – just one beamed at her, because she had really perceived him.

'I see,' Sophia thought, 'not only rich people are blind. It can happen to poor people, as well!'

And she roamed through the big city. Almost no one looked up, hardly anyone noticed the other. Just now and then, her eyes met those of someone with a perceptive heart, and they smiled at each other like old friends.

Finally, she reached the forest at the peripheries. The birds were singing and the sun shone. Sophia felt her burden lift. Blissful, she sat down under a tree and enjoyed the calm, the warm sun and the slight breeze. But after a while something bothered her.

She turned and found, that she had been sitting on a pointed stone. When she took it up and inspected it more closely, she noticed, that it was a special stone. 'Oh, a rose quartz!' Sophia exclaimed, amazed. As a princess, she was an expert on those things.

'This is not simply a rose quartz!' a voice sounded above her. Surprised, Sophia looked up, but couldn't see a soul – no one but an owl sitting on a branch above her.

'Is there anybody?' Sophia shouted.

'Am I nobody?' the owl asked in return.

Sophia thought, someone was making fun of her.

'Animals cannot speak!' she said aloud to herself.

'Of course, they can!' the owl bristled. 'It's just, that humans can usually not understand us, because they think, that animals have no soul and are inferior to them. But the stone that you are holding in your hand opens your heart to the language of the animals. Take good care of it – you will need it again!'

'Oh, will I be allowed to keep this wonderstone?' Sophia asked, surprised.

'Obviously!' the owl replied. 'Since it lay there especially for you. It shall accompany you on your way to the Land of the Perceptive Hearts.'

'How do you know, that I'm in search of this land?' Sophia asked.

'Very simply, because only seekers can recognize this love-stone as precious. To all others it looks quite ordinary,' the owl answered. 'Have a good trip!'

Thus Sophia continued on her way.

Suddenly, she heard a loud, agitated quacking and when she followed the sound, she found a mother-duck hopelessly entangled in a blackberry bush, who tried in vain to free herself by flapping her wings wildly.

Her ducklings bustled about, cheeping in panic in front of the bush. Sophia talked at the little ones soothingly. Then she said to the mother-duck: 'Trust me! Don't move. Otherwise, I cannot help you.'

After a great deal of reassuring, the mother-duck calmed down, and Sophia succeeded in freeing her carefully from the bush, although not entirely unscathed.

Gently, Sophia picked the ducklings up on one arm, the mother-duck on the other, and took them to the nearby pond, which she had seen through the bushes. There, she let the mother-duck down first, and then the little ones. Grateful, the family slipped into the water.

'As a special thank-you for your help,' the mother-duck said, 'I will tell you a secret: In the woods beyond this pond, there is a tree with golden fruit that are never eaten up. When you take a bite off one, the gap fills instantly. Thus, you always have enough to eat. Besides, the fruit always has the taste you wish for, and if someone is sick and eats of it, he or she will be well again right away. Have a good trip!'

Sophia thanked her overjoyed, for in the meantime she had become quite hungry. She found the tree and plucked a fruit. It tasted delicious and, sure enough, it did not become less. Strengthened, Sophia continued on her way. When she turned around, she could not detect the tree with the golden fruit anymore – it had disappeared.

As she walked cheerfully through the woods, she suddenly heard a howling. She followed the sound, and found a fox, whose paw was pinched in a leghold trap. He suffered great pain, and howled and whimpered piteously.

'Wait, I'll help you,' Sophia promised and tried to pull the leghold trap apart. It was jammed tightly, and with great effort she could only open it a little bit.

'Quickly! Pull your paw out of it, before it snaps shut again!' Sophia panted. The fox understood her and was free, but his paw looked terrible and hurt. Sophia remembered, that her fruit was supposed to have a healing effect. So she bit off a piece, and gave it to the fox to eat. And, lo and behold, his wound healed in no time at all.

Gratefully the fox took her to his den and disappeared within. After a while, he returned with a pair of golden shoes and said: 'Because you have helped me, I give you these special shoes. Whoever wears them, can walk as far as she wants, without ever tiring.'

'Oh, how very practical!' Sophia exclaimed full of joy, for she had become quite exhausted from her long walk. The shoes fit, as if they had been made for her. She thanked the fox and moved on.

Unnoticed by Sophia, a thunderstorm had come up in the meantime, and darkness fell. Before she knew it, she got into heavy rainfall. It was blowing a gale and she could barely see her hand in front of her face. She fought the wind and the rain, and took shelter under a big tree, but the rain came from everywhere. So she continued on her way, hoping to find better shelter.

As she crossed the forest, more staggering than walking, she suddenly detected a small light not far from her. She headed towards it, and found a little cottage. She knocked. Once, twice and once again. Nothing moved. Sophia shouted. At last, the door opened, an old woman standing in the doorway.

'More haste, less speed,' she grumbled. Then she admitted Sophia, who was soaked and chilled to the bone, into the house.

'What are you doing in the forest in this weather?' the woman asked indignantly. Sophia sneezed.

'Well, then take off your wet clothes and wrap this blanket around yourself,' the woman said somewhat friendlier now.

A merry fire was burning in the fireplace, and Sophia was allowed to sit down in front of it in her blanket. Gradually she warmed up.

'I'm searching for the Land of the Perceptive Hearts,' she answered.

'Then you have come to the right place!' the woman said. 'If you stay with me, and help me as long as I need you, I shall give you a map that will lead you directly there. But you better rest now.' She laid out a second blanket in front of the fireplace and motioned her to lay down there. Sophia fell asleep at once.

When she awoke, the old woman was already up, preparing breakfast. Sophia put on her dry clothes and asked: 'What am I supposed to do for you?'

'Everything in its own good time!' the woman replied. So they ate their breakfast in silence, although Sophia was bursting with questions: who the woman was, what she did in the middle of the forest, why she was all alone, how she knew about the Land of the Perceptive Hearts and much more.

After breakfast, the woman had Sophia fetch water in the nearby lake. The weather had calmed down. Sophia took two large buckets and set out. She found the lake and carried the two buckets filled with water back to the house. She had to go three times. Then she was sent into the forest to gather wood for the fireplace. When she came home at last, a tub with washing waited for her, to be done. The fire had to be kept going and the house to be cleaned. And before Sophia knew it, the day was done and she hadn't asked any of her questions.

The next day, the same procedure was repeated, and also on the following one. At last Sophia mustered the courage to ask: 'How much longer am I supposed to do all this? When will I get the map to the Land of the Perceptive Hearts?'

'One step at a time!' the woman answered. 'You will have to stay as long as I need you.'

'How long will that be?' Sophia inquired.

'You will know, when it is time for you to move on,' the woman replied.

Thus Sophia stayed with the old woman and helped her, as best as she could. Every now and then she was overcome by doubts, whether this was the right way of achieving her goal, but the woman insisted on her staying and working for her. Day in, day out the same work. It was often dreary and always wearisome. Sometimes Sophia was about to forget about her intent.

Sophia often dreamed about simply walking off and leaving everything behind. At times she revolted.

*So one day the old woman handed her a book and told her: 'The path you are searching, for leads inwards. Read in this book a little every day, and you will find it. Apart from that, do your work faithfully, wait and see.'*

*Time went by, and Sophia wasn't sure, if it were weeks, months or years. She read in that book of wisdom daily, and it filled her with joy and hope for the land, she was searching for. She did her work and often thought: 'What a waste of time!', but she didn't dare say it aloud.*

*One day, after quite some time – Sophia had long since given up hope – the woman took her aside and said: 'Since you have persevered even in work, which you didn't enjoy, I will now explain to you, what purpose it served: All along, you have been walking the path you came searching for. It made you more patient and mature and has brought you closer to your goal, without your realizing it.'*

*'Will I get that map now?' Sophia asked excitedly.*

*The old woman smiled: 'The map,' she said, 'is always the person next to you. Each person you meet, will lead you further on your path, will show you more about the world, about him or herself and about you yourself. Once you learn to perceive the true reality behind the outer appearances, you will find yourself in the Land of the Perceptive Hearts.*

Return home now, into your castle. Your apprenticeship with me is over. Take your love-stone, the golden fruit, the golden shoes and the book of wisdom back with you, for your journey is not yet over.'

Sophia bid farewell to the woman and cheerfully set out for home. Because of her special gifts, the golden fruit and the book of wisdom, she always had nourishment for body and soul, by the use of her golden shoes, she didn't tire on her path, and the love-stone made her visible for the people she met, for it opened their hearts to her.

She came through many villages and cities, and she understood the people, who had to work so hard to make a living for themselves and others. She talked to many of them, and shared in their worries and joys. She began to truly perceive the people crossing her path, and was perceived herself, with pleasure.

When she finally arrived at home, she saw an elderly gentleman sitting in the sun in front of the castle taking a nap.

'Mr. Joy!' Sophia shouted happily and broke into a run.

Mr. Joy raised his head, and his eyes lit up, when he recognized Sophia.

Many years had passed, and Sophia had in the meantime become a young lady.

Mr. Joy was beaming from ear to ear: 'I have been waiting for you, Sophia. I knew you would soon return.' They embraced each other affectionately.

'But I have not found the Land of the Perceptive Hearts and the Golden Cloak, you were talking about.'

'Yes, you have,' Mr. Joy smiled, 'for this land is within and the Golden Cloak is the Cloak of Love and Compassion that is woven by Life itself. It will help you to perceive people as they really are, and will protect you from injuries by people, who have merely been injured themselves.

If you perceive people through the eyes of love, you will also be perceived yourself – but then it will not be that important to you anymore.'

Together, they entered the castle. The news of the princess' return spread like wildfire. Everyone was amazed and full of joy at seeing her – even her parents, who had always been busy and hadn't made time for her, before she had left. There were tears of joy and lots of talking and laughing.

Some years later, Sophia's parents passed the state affairs on to her and retired, for they saw, what a wise and prudent woman she had become.

Sophia selected a circle of women and men, who also walked the Path of the Heart, and who helped and counseled her, concerning the state affairs.

She sent messengers among her people, to question them, what they needed, and what they would do differently, if they were ruling the country.

Every now and then, princes from other countries came, to propose to her, but Sophia saw, that they were interested in material things only, and did not share in her world. She never found a kindred soul like Mr. Joy again.

Sophia ruled well and with pleasure, and the Cloak of Love and Compassion provided valuable service to her.

After many, many years, when it became time for her to leave the world, she appointed a capable woman and a man equally wise from her circle of friends and counselors, who were capable of continuing the state affairs in a modern way. Thus, the country witnessed a long period of peace and prosperity, and as long as the Path of the Heart is cherished, things will remain that way.

# Life Is a Symphony

*There was once a very lonely tone. The other tones of his family were pretty much in harmony, and sounded as one – only he didn't quite fit in.*

*The other family members made no secret of the fact, that they did not appreciate his sound, and so he hardly ever dared to ring out. But what is a tone, if he is not ringing out?*

*Thus, the lonely tone decided to move away from his family. He roamed about, ringing here and there, but he couldn't find any meaning in it.*

*'What are tones in the world for?' he asked himself.*

*By chance, he passed a tree, on which a bird was chirping cheerfully. This impressed the wandering tone very much, and he tentatively began to ring out.*

*'Oh, how beautiful you are!' the bird chirped. 'You have been missing in my melody!' And it happily blared the tone out into the world. For the first time in his life, the tone got to hear his full sound.*

*'How beautiful I am!' he rejoiced. 'Thank you, dear bird, for showing me.'*

*'I thank you,' the bird replied. 'You have enriched my song!'*

*In high spirits, the tone moved on. It was not long, before he happened upon a musician, who was creating a new melody.*

Inspired by all those other tones, our tone dared to ring out, as well – very cautiously at first, but then more and more courageously.

'How wonderful!' the musician exclaimed. 'You have been missing in my melody!'

And he assigned the tone his place in the new piece of music. How happy this made the tone! Finally, he could be of use to someone. And he sounded more beautiful, than ever before in his life.

The musician became his close friend, and therefore he dared to ask him the question of his life:

'What are tones in the world for? They sound and fade away, and no one thinks about them anymore.'

'This is, how it may appear to one tone alone,' the musician replied. 'But come with me! Let me show you something.'

And thus, the musician took the tone with him to his orchestra. There were so many tones ringing out there, like our tone had never before experienced. Shyly, he held back.

'You have to ring out!' his friend, the musician, shouted. 'Otherwise something is missing in our music. A tone is only alive, when he sounds. Life is a symphony! Every single tone is important! If one does not ring out, the others cannot make up for it, and the work remains incomplete.'

*Thus, our tone took heart and rang out, sometimes with the violins, sometimes with the trumpets, then again with the flutes - and soon bounced cheerfully all through the orchestra, just like all the other tones. It was a real joy!*

*At last, he could feel, what tones are in the world for.*

# The Clown's Secret

*There was once a circus clown. Everybody just cracked up, when he put on his show, and even apart from that, he always had a joke on his lips. He was well known, far and wide, for his apt remarks, which he put forth with love and humor. At all times he wore a friendly smile on his face and was well-liked.*

*But when he returned to his trailer, he was often seized with a deep sadness, and it was not unusual for him to start crying – of course, nobody was supposed to know of it.*

*Only a little mouse, who had right of residence with him, regularly witnessed the drama.*

*'Why are you crying so much?' it finally asked him one day.*

*'I'm not sure myself,' the clown sobbed. 'For others, I have nothing but laughter and cheerfulness, but there is none of it left for me, and so I fall into a deep hole, when I am alone, and feel very sad.'*

*'Couldn't you save up some of your laughter, so that there would be enough left for yourself?' the mouse asked him. 'If you gave me all your cheese and would not save any, you would have to starve!'*

*'That's true,' the clown conceded, 'but if I hold back my laughter, people won't like me anymore.'*

'If you have no laughter left for yourself, you will soon have none left for anybody!' the mouse warned him.

Thus the clown started to go around, not always laughing and joking, but sometimes serious and pensive.

People immediately noticed the difference and were surprised. 'In a bad mood today?' they asked and added: 'Looks like somebody rubbed you up the wrong way!'

He smiled at them in his friendly manner, and said nothing. They wouldn't have understood him. After a while, though, the circus director noticed it, too, that his clown wasn't cheerful anymore at all times, and he became concerned. A serious clown is not good for business after all. He summoned the clown and said:

'I hear, that you are not as funny anymore as you have always been. This needs to change again. People do not want to see a serious clown, but want to be able to laugh about him.'

The clown answered: 'I do my very best, but do I always have to wear my clown-mask? Won't I be allowed to show my serious side at times?'

'That's not, what you are here for!' the circus director replied. 'You either make people laugh or you are fired!'

Despondent, the clown returned to his trailer. 'Here you are!' he said to the mouse. 'A serious clown is not worth anything!'

'You are a valuable person – not only, when you are funny,' the mouse objected, 'and if not everyone can see this, it is not necessarily your fault. I'm sure, there are people, who will recognize you for what you really are – if not here, then elsewhere. Go searching for them.'

The clown brooded and brooded for days. His mood and health declined. Finally he made his decision and went to see the circus director.

'I cannot keep denying my true Self. It kills me to always have to be cheerful. If I am not allowed to take off my clown-mask at times, I will have to leave,' he told him.

The circus director just looked at him blankly. After a while he answered: 'If that's, what you wish, I guess you'll have to leave.'

So the clown packed his bundle, said farewell to the wise mouse and his colleagues and set forth to find people, with whom he would be allowed to really remain himself, whether he laughed or cried.

He came through many towns and villages. Everywhere he performed his buffooneries, and thus earned a living. He found shelter under bridges or trees at night. Sometimes, he was allowed to sleep in *a barn, too, or he was even offered proper quarters, because he had brought so much joy to the people.*

*He experienced many things on his journeys: Things beautiful or terrible, interesting or peculiar, remarkable or ordinary. And although he had formerly also got around quite a bit, he now learned much more about other people and the world in general. Whenever he felt like it, he could now put his clown-mask aside and think about everything, without having to consider his effect on others, for he was all by himself.*

*One day, when he had finished his performance, the cheering people standing or sitting around him called for an encore. They couldn't get enough. So he came up with the idea of telling stories from his life: Stories cheerful or sad, thrilling or entertaining, probable or improbable.*

*People listened interestedly and were fascinated. They laughed and cried, cheered and marveled, because he related his stories so vividly.*

*After he had thus discovered his talent for story-telling, he had to put on his show less and less often, because, when he had finished relating his stories, people were so touched, that they generously provided him with everything he needed. Thus he could present every aspect of his person, without anyone taking offense, and he didn't have to hide behind a mask of fake cheerfulness anymore.*

One day, he came into some village again, to tell his stories, when he noticed a man among the listeners, who looked at him in a benign and approving manner. After he had ended, this man came to him and asked him:

'Are you feeling alright as a vagabond – no shelter, no home?'

'Well,' the clown answered, 'sometimes, I long for a home, indeed, but what I am really looking for, are people, who recognize me for what I am! Up till now I have had much applause, but nobody has ever really perceived me as I am as a person.'

'There is someone, who knows you inside out, and who looks behind all masks,' the man said. 'He, too, is a great story-teller. He, too, knows the homeless wandering about, and the search for being perceived and understood.'

The clown looked at him full of hope: 'You are the first person to understand my yearning!'

'Come with me,' the man replied, 'maybe you will find, what you are looking for; otherwise, you can simply move on.'

The man turned out to be the pastor of the village, and he took the clown with him to the parsonage. There, he was allowed to take a bath, dress in new clothes, and he received a delicious meal. After all this time, he finally found someone, who he could unburden his heart to. The pastor really listened to him and, after the clown had finished, he said:

'Our parish clerk has recently died. Would you like to take over his job?'

The clown was overwhelmed. After a long pause, he answered:

'It would be great, to have a real home for once, and not to have to be on the move all the time. I finally found a person, who perceives me. How grateful I would be, if I were allowed to stay!'

Thus the clown began a regular life. It was some change for him, who had been travelling around for all of his life, but he enjoyed it.

Since he had had so many interesting experiences and was a fantastic story-teller, the pastor used him in his church services, as well. The clown learned all about the other 'great story-teller', who had travelled around, to tell people about God's love for them, by making up ever new parables, which people could understand.

The clown, too, was a master hereof and thus brought the pastor's sermons to life. They became a perfect team: The pastor interpreted the Bible and the clown told lively stories to illustrate the point, the pastor was trying to make, so that people would understand more easily.

*But even though the clown liked it in the parsonage, and felt comfortable, with time he got more and more restless. The pastor noticed his growing unrest and asked him for the reason.*

*'I feel comfortable here,' the clown answered, 'but as much as I enjoy the fellowship in the parsonage, it also constricts me. I need my freedom! I want to move on again.'*

*'Are you sure?' the pastor inquired. 'Could it be, that you are searching without for something. that you can only find within?'*

*'What do you mean?' the clown asked, baffled.*

*'What kind of freedom are you talking about?' the pastor probed. 'Do you mean the freedom to be yourself, or the freedom of all rules and compromises, which are simply necessary for living together?*

*In the first case you could stay with us. We would provide lodging for you in the extension of the parsonage, where you could retreat, to have more quiet time to turn within, so you could discover your true essence. For this kind of freedom has to grow within you, and is possible even in a fellowship. If, however, you oppose playing by the rules of the fellowship, you will have to move on. This would mean, that you prefer staying alone at all costs.'*

*'I've never seen it that way,' the clown said pensively. 'I always thought, to be free, you'd have to be alone!'*

A fellowship not only constricts you – it also supports you,' the pastor pointed out. 'What is it, that makes you feel constricted in a fellowship?'

'I always have the feeling of having to wear a mask, to be accepted,' the clown replied. 'There are very few people, with whom I dare to show myself as I am. With all others I think, that they would despise me if I did.'

'Why do you think that?' the pastor pressed on.

'It has been my experience, whenever I didn't meet the expectations,' the clown stated.

'Just because some people have formerly reacted that way, this doesn't mean, everybody will. And even if some do, it doesn't mean that it is justified. Could it be that you despise yourself? That you doubt your own value?'

'I often do!' the clown admitted.

'Many people do,' the pastor said sympathetically. 'That is no reason to despair, and no reason to flee. What changes for you, if you wander about by yourself?'

'Then I feel at home within myself and am accountable to none,' the clown answered.

'Maybe, all you need, is to take one step back. Let us try the following,' the pastor suggested, 'you move into the extension of the parsonage for about half a *year and take all the freedom, you need. You can travel around or retreat to your room for quiet inner reflection. You are released from your duty for that time and have to answer to none. If you long for company, you are welcome to join us, but you then have to conform to the rules of the fellowship.*

*The rest of the time you live all alone. After that period you decide, whether you still want to move on. Maybe, by that time you will have found, what you are searching for.'*

*'I'm not even sure, what it is, I am searching for,' the clown replied.*

*'Maybe, we are all searching, all throughout our lives, for what really makes us, who we are – our essence, our Self,' the pastor pondered aloud.*

*'Isn't it selfish to search for one's Self?' the clown wanted to know.*

*'I rather believe, that selfishness develops, if you don't love your Self, because in that case, everything focusses on the need to fill that inner void you feel,' the pastor reasoned.*

*Thus the clown moved into the extension of the parsonage. But he didn't stay long. He took up his roving again. For weeks, he travelled around through regions, where he was unknown, and took shelter under bridges, trees or in barns again. But this wandering about aimlessly, that he had glorified in his memory, was anything but romantic. He didn't feel free, but felt unsafe and uncomfortable – now that he knew the alternative. He remembered the pastor's sentence: 'Could it be, that you are searching without for something, that you can only find within?'*

*So he returned to the parsonage again, that had become home to him, to turn inward. Day after day he took quiet time from then on. He didn't want to see anyone.*

*When one day he sat in his room again – with closed eyes, without any distractions – he suddenly had the feeling of falling into a deep well, deep and deeper. Fear took hold of him. He wanted to stop the fall, for he didn't know what expected him. But he heard a voice whisper deep within: 'Let go!'*

*Time seemed to stand still. Deeper and deeper he fell into the darkness of the well. When he reached the water surface, he beheld an indescribably beautiful, huge blossom bud unfolding. And his inner voice said: 'What you are seeing, is your Self.'*

*Tears rolled down his cheeks, when he opened his eyes. He sat still and let his experience sink in.*

*He never told anybody about it, for it was so precious and holy – words would have destroyed it. But his demeanor changed, and it was obvious to everyone, who knew him, that something very special had happened to him.*

*Shortly afterwards, the former clown took up his work as parish clerk again, and returned into the fellowship. He became quieter, was more at peace with himself and didn't have to put on a show anymore, for now he knew his true value.*

# Be Yourself

Some time ago, there was a young birch tree, which stood near a tree nursery, where firs were grown, that would one day serve as Christmas trees. The birch often overheard the fir trees enthusiastically talking among themselves about, how it would be, to stand in a living room, beautifully decorated, bringing joy to people.

They imagined, how the children would adorn them with candy and decoration, and how the whole family would honor them and focus all their attention on them. They had heard this from the birds, which often peered into the windows of people and knew about their ways.

The young birch tree dreamed about becoming a Christmas tree one day. She didn't want to just stand in the grove with the other birches, because it made her feel so insignificant. Thus, she persistently practiced to arrange her leaves in parallel order like fir needles. The other birches were completely baffled.

Once, when people passed by the birch grove, they stood in front of the young birch and laughed: 'It sure looks funny! What's wrong with its leaves?'

This made the young birch feel very ashamed. An old, wise birch tree standing nearby encouraged her: 'Don't pretend to be like someone else. Be, who you truly are, with pride!'

'But I feel so insignificant!' the young birch complained.

'You need to understand,' the wise birch tree returned, 'that there is no such thing as an insignificant creature. Everyone is important for the Whole, wherever she may find herself. You need not compare yourself with others – because it is only then, that you feel insignificant. Just be yourself!

Look at your beautiful white trunk shining in the moonlight. Sway your airy crown with the breeze. Rejoice in the gifts, you can bring to the world.

Thus the young birch tree shook out her leaves, that she had been rigidly holding parallel, in order to look like a fir tree, and relaxed. She felt lighter and became aware, how her saps and energies were now flowing more freely. Joy filled her, and she savored the gentle breeze rustling her leaves.

Over time, she grew to be so gorgeous, that she became the most beautiful birch in the grove, the pride of all. But she was not aware of it, and did not care anymore.

At Christmas time, the young firs were cut down and loaded to become Christmas trees. Even if this was the highlight, it was also the end of their lives. And the birch was grateful now, that she was not a fir tree!

# The Global Merry-Go-Round

There was once a merry-go-round that was ridden mainly by adults, rather than children. They rode on "Work", "Money" and "Power" – or whatever they called their figures. There were also smaller figures, called "Family" or "Pleasures".

In the center of the merry-go-round a huge so-called "CleverTel" was rotating, attracting all the attention, because there was at all times something funny or horrible or meaningless happening on its screen.

Everyone revolved around this central point. They watched mesmerized. From its speakers emanated an incessant stream of so-called "information", instead of beautiful music, because that was, what the people on the merry-go-round wanted to listen to.

The merry-go-round rotated faster and faster. People, who didn't hold on to their figures very firmly, were mercilessly hurled out of it. Then one of the spectators outside the merry-go-round could, if he was quick, jump up and try his luck.

Life was easier on those riding on figures more in the center, like "Power" and "Money", than on those riding on "Work", more on the periphery. People in the center weren't flung around as much and not as easily hurled from their figures. Sometimes, however, someone from the periphery would try to push one of them off his figure and mount it himself.

*The spectators in front of the merry-go-round watched the scene presenting to them, some wanting to be part of it, others shaking their heads in incredulous amazement at the madness taking place before their eyes.*

*Both groups comprised children and elderly people, as well as those, who had been hurled out of the merry-go-round. One part of them tried to get back on, a second part retreated, saddened, while a third part had a light-bulb moment, when watching the goings-on, and started searching for alternatives. They tried to break loose from the all-dominant "Clever-Tel" to feel out and pursue their own values.*

*It was very hard to choose a path beyond the merry-go-round and escape the hypnotic effect of the "CleverTel". This was also a very lonely path, for – even if more and more people found it – the masses did not walk it. Whoever needed their approval, had to try to keep pace with the merry-go-round, even if it should cost his life.*

*One fine day the merry-go-round suddenly came to a halt with a jolt. Almost all of those riding along tumbled off their figures – just a very few in the inner circle of "Power" remained seated on their figures.*

*But the bewildered people having fallen off, were much too busy with picking themselves up and examining their injuries to notice this.*

Many of those, who had been watching from afar, came to care for the dazed and injured people.

Meanwhile the merry-go-round slowly started rotating again with only the people in the inner circle still holding on to their figures. Shame on him who thinks evil upon it.

They continued circling as if nothing had happened, not even deigning to look at the people that had fallen off.

Some of those people, though, instead of trying to get on again, started to question the global merry-go-round. They began to reflect on issues like:

Do I really want to continue living like that?

What is important to me?

What makes me feel good?

Questions that had always been stifled in the daily routine.

So, while some of those, having fallen off, were still looking longingly towards the merry-go-round, which they couldn't ride anymore due to their injuries, others started to think about alternatives to their previous way of life.

Gratefully they turned towards those, who had helped them after the fall, and who hadn't been able to ride the merry-go-round for quite some time. Together they created visions of a loving and joyous *fellowship, in which nobody was neglected, everyone was treated fairly, and truth had top priority.*

*Soon, they had forgotten about the "powers that be", who were still rotating on their merry-go-round.*

*But if no one rides the merry-go-round anymore, these soon realized, there is no one left to exercise power over.*

*The "powers that be" scratched their heads. Something seemed to have gone wrong. They had expected to increase their power, by graciously allowing some of the humiliated fallen people back onto the merry-go-round. But now that more and more people refused to be controlled by the "CleverTel" any longer, they saw their hopes dashed.*

*Meanwhile, the news, that many people on Earth were not living on the merry-go-round anymore, had reached even distant worlds, and many spiritually advanced people from those worlds came to help the dropouts in building a new society – albeit only as help for helping themselves.*

*The former "powers that be" tried to sabotage this development wherever they could. They made every effort to decoy, threaten and manipulate, but their long-established methods didn't work anymore with most people. These had broken the chains of their seeming dependency and were exploring new avenues.*

The people thus liberated left the large cities with their mass housing, and built smaller settlements with manageable housing units, in which families and individuals, young and old lived together in a colorful mix.

They formed small groups that shared everything, and in which everyone made their contribution to the common good, even those, who had not been able to ride the merry-go-round for a long time, and had been considered "useless" to society.

Everyone was allowed to do what they did best, and what gave them pleasure. Thus, everyone enjoyed working and their communities flourished. Money was no longer necessary, because everyone got what they needed and longed for. There was enough of everything for everybody, because everyone used their talents for the benefit of others.

Everyone was also allowed to learn everything, they wanted to know and be able to do, regardless of age and status. For this purpose, there were academies everywhere, where you could practice and develop your skills and talents.

People were now guided and advised by the wisest members of the communities – not the most ambitious ones – and by the mentors from other worlds, who withdrew, though, as soon as the new communities were functioning adequately.

*The former powers were assigned a separate, ulterior region, which they could arrange according to their wishes, but only with those people, who wished to join them voluntarily. They were prevented from harassing and interfering with the people of good will in their new communities.*

*Since the latter could now evolve unimpeded, and everyone was allowed to live according to the abilities and needs inherent in their nature, they all learned to live together in love, peace and harmony.*

*Hatred, envy and quarrels were soon forgotten, because no one suffered any want. Everyone was feeling fine, and no one ever thought about times gone by anymore.*

# Lost & Found

*Once upon a time, there was a maid named Elisa. She had served her landlord faithfully for many a year. He understood his business and, though his servants had often enough known hard times, his land supported all, who were working for him in the house and the fields.*

*When the manor was taken over by a new owner one day, things started to go downhill. The fields and meadows didn't yield sufficient crops anymore, and the owner, who attributed this to his lazy and inept maids and menials, laid all of them off. With a small band of followers, he wanted to do a better job than the old landlord.*

*Elisa, who wasn't so young anymore, was scared of her future, for it didn't look too bright. Her worrying and brooding over, how to make a living in a world, where only the young and strong counted, made her sick. At night she couldn't sleep anymore.*

*When she opened her breadbox one morning to eat up her last piece of dry bread, she found a beautiful golden ring with a sparkling jewel within. Amazed and overjoyed about this unexpected find – which was so gorgeous – she forgot about her misery, for she had never seen anything like it. Happily she put the ring on her finger. If fit perfectly.*

*The burden fell off her heart and she thought: 'Now I don't have to worry anymore. I will simply sell this ring. It is probably worth a fortune.'*

*She went downtown to the jeweler to show him her treasure. He only looked at her dumbfounded, though. What Elisa didn't know: It was a very special ring – not everyone could see it, for it was made of gold produced by dwarfs. Thus the jeweler, who couldn't see it, thought that she was out of her mind.*

*Disappointed, she made for home. When she passed the market, she wanted to hurry past, for she had no money for all those delightful goods one could buy there. There were fruit from all over the world, the sweetest pastries, nice baskets, clothing and much more. Sadly she wanted to turn away, when a market woman addressed her in a friendly manner:*

*'Hello, Elisa. I have a basket with specialties for the Master Behind the Woods. Would you like to take them there? You would benefit from it, too, you know.*

*Elisa asked surprised: 'Where do you know me from?'*

*The market woman only smiled mysteriously and inquired: 'Are you willing to?'*

*Elisa hesitated: 'I don't like to go through the forest all by myself. It is dangerous and I get lost easily.'*

*'Don't worry,' the friendly market woman replied, 'you have your ring. It will help you through any difficulties. Have faith!'*

Elisa thought about it: She had time, since she had lost her job, and maybe new opportunities would arise with this errand. So she decided to risk it.

It all seemed kind of odd – the strange woman, who knew her name and knew of her ring, and that assignment – but she conquered her fears and accepted.

'Strengthen yourself, before you go. Take whatever fruit you like from my stall, for it is a long way to go,' the market woman offered her.

Elisa didn't need to be told twice. Oh, how delicious and sweet, all those different fruit, one more tasty than the other. With every bite she took, Elisa's mood improved and hope and confidence returned. But eventually it was time for her to leave.

Elisa took the basket with the specialties for the Master Behind the Woods, received some food for herself and bravely set out.

In answer to her question, how she was to find the Master, the market woman had only referred her to her ring. Somewhat insecurely Elisa walked through the city towards the forest edge.

At the first fork on her path, she stretched out her hand with the ring, hoping that her arm would be pulled into the right direction. But nothing of the sort happened. Without a clue, she looked around. Once again she stretched out her arm. Suddenly, a little blue butterfly landed on her hand. She was watching it with delight, when it took off and fluttered to a flower on the right side of the fork.

'Well,' Elisa thought, 'maybe this is the sign I was looking for. I will simply continue into this direction.'

Thus, she followed the path deeper into the forest. At the next fork, she tried her luck with the ring once more, and again nothing happened. After a while she sat down on a boulder at the wayside and brooded about, what to do.

A little squirrel came close, full of curiosity, and sniffed at her hand. She opened her food-bag and offered it something. It was funny to watch it eat. Gratefully it rubbed its head at Elisa's ring and jumped off cheerfully along the path.

And again, Elisa decided to take this as a sign and followed it. She continued in that manner, whenever she wasn't sure about which path to take. Again and again, she found a sign to show her the way.

Gradually it was getting dark and Elisa could not make out her goal far and wide. The Master, she was looking for, was supposed to live behind the forest in a hut with an herb garden. She was to recognize the hut by its sparking chimney. So the market woman had told her.

Soon it was so dark that Elisa couldn't see her hand in front of her face. The trees were standing close together and she bumped into more than one.

There was no way, she could go on. This was not, what she had bargained for. Long since, should she have delivered her basket and have been back home.

In the forest she heard eerie noises. It crackled, rustled and howled around her and she got frightened. She couldn't escape. What should she do? Desperate, she sat down under a tree and wept bitterly.

Suddenly the ring, she wore on her finger, started to glow. It lit up the immediate surroundings, so that she could see something again. She got up, and continued on her way, further into the forest. The light just illuminated the next step – and then another one.

All at once, she saw another light gleam through the bushes and trees. She headed for it. The light came out of a cave. Cautiously she entered. Therein, she found a number of dwarfs, working diligently underground. It took them a while to notice Elisa. But her glowing ring finally caught their attention. One of the dwarfs greeted her warmly:

'Welcome, dear human! We have been waiting for you.'

Elisa was surprised: 'You have been waiting for me?'

'We sent you the ring, so you would find us,' the dwarf replied. 'What can we do for you?'

Trustingly, she told him, how she had lost her work and therefore had taken on an assignment, to bring a basket full of specialties to the Master Behind the

Woods, but that she couldn't find her way in the dark, and had become very much scared of the unknown noises in the sinister forest. She didn't know what to do.

'Don't worry,' the dwarf comforted her. 'Come and rest, first of all.'

He led her into the back of the cave, and showed her a place, where she could retreat to. Exhausted, as she was, she soon fell asleep.

When she awoke, she felt refreshed and took heart again. The dwarfs cared for her very kindly and then guided Elisa proudly through their workshop, where many of them were diligently at work, some digging for gold, others melting it, and yet others creating the most beautiful jewelry from it.

Every single one of them, was a master of his trade and each one needed the others and appreciated their contributions, so that the whole could be successful.

With the finished jewelry, they helped humans above-ground, who were in need, for dwarfs have no use for gold – they are cared for by Mother Earth.

As a farewell-present the dwarfs gave Elisa a precious diadem from their workshop. 'Whenever you are confused and don't know, what to do, it will help you to clear your thoughts and find new ways,' one of the dwarfs explained the gift to her. She was overwhelmed and thanked them cordially.

After the dwarfs had refilled her food supplies, they led her back to the cave entrance, and gave her directions to her destination. She bid farewell to the friendly dwarfs and set out full of confidence.

Cheerfully, she strode ahead, and by noon she had covered quite a distance. Suddenly, there was a rustling noise, branches cracked and all at once, a huge, shaggy monster stood in front of her, snarling and hissing angrily. Paralyzed with terror, she stopped dead in her tracks. The monster blocked her way.

She couldn't think straight anymore. Cautiously, she backed off. The monster advanced towards her. She turned to her right – he followed suit. To the left – she couldn't evade him – he was following her every move.

At last, she felt the effect of her wonderful diadem and her thoughts cleared. She remembered, that if you are threatened by a wild animal, you are not supposed to show fear. She mustered all her courage and shouted: 'Stop! No further!' defensively holding up her hand with the ring. The monster was bewildered, and simply sat down.

'And now, what?' Elisa thought. Then she remembered her food-bag. Slowly, without taking her eyes off the monster, she opened it, took out some of the goodies, and threw them his way. Greedily he lunged for them and drew nearer. Elisa took another piece and threw it further away. But the monster instantly came back and advanced towards that interesting bag. He suddenly didn't appear that monstrous anymore, but quite gentle.

When Elisa took the next piece out of her bag, he didn't wait, but ate it out of her hand. Elisa took heart and tentatively ruffled his fur. He obviously enjoyed that. Thus they became friends.

Elisa set out again. Her new friend followed on her heels. Together they roamed through the forest, enjoying the sun and the birdsong. It was just beautiful.

After a while, though, Elisa lost her confidence: Were they still going into the right direction? In the bright sunlight and because of the trees, she couldn't make out the sparking chimney of the hut belonging to the Master Behind the Woods, although it couldn't be very far anymore. The monster, turning up so unexpectedly, had distracted her so much, that she hadn't paid attention to the way and had lost her bearings.

In the distance, she heard a mighty rushing. Her monstrous friend trotted friskily towards it.

Elisa followed hesitantly. The rushing swelled into a roar, and suddenly the two of them stood in front of a rapid stream. How should they get to the other side? They walked along the bank of the river, hoping to find a way across – in vain.

*While Elisa was still brooding about how to proceed, her monstrous friend got all excited and was about to jump into the water.*

*'Don't!' Elisa shouted. 'That is too dangerous!'*

*But her friend nudged her into the water and jumped after her. Unexpectedly enough, the water was warm, but very wild, and Elisa sank.*

*Suddenly she felt something shaggy at her side, and held on for dear life. Her friend helped her safely through the torrent to the other bank, where both of them had to catch their breath first.*

*Appalled, Elisa noticed, that she had lost the basket with the specialties for the Master Behind the Woods. What should she tell him?*

*As night was falling, she could now make out the sparking chimney of his hut, but she had nothing to bring anymore. Worried and a bit scared, too, she approached the hut. Its windows were lit by a warm light from within, and when she came closer, the Master stepped in front of the hut.*

*'Hello, Elisa,' he greeted her warmly, 'I am happy to meet you.'*

*Elisa didn't have to ask him, whether he was the Master, she had been searching for – she knew, she had reached her goal.*

Dejected, she told him: 'I am very sorry, but I have lost the basket with the specialties, I was supposed to deliver to you, on the last part of the way. I have failed.'

'No, you haven't,' the Master smiled. 'It was not about the basket. I don't need anything.'

'Then why did I have to go through all this trouble?' Elisa demanded tiredly.

'What I am interested in,' the Master answered, 'is, that you yourself have come to me, for you shall from now on work for me, if you wish.'

'What could I possibly do, that would be of use to you?' Elisa asked timidly.

'You shall be my messenger from now on, and keep up the communication between me and the City in Front of the Woods. But come and rest first. We will talk about it tomorrow.'

Thus Elisa found new work and her desperate situation took a turn for the better. From then on, she kept bringing gifts and messages from the Master Behind the Woods to the City.

The path soon became familiar to her and wasn't as hazardous anymore, as the first time. The dwarfs' gold – her ring and the diadem – helped her to handle any difficulties. She was well off with her Master and enjoyed serving him. He was most kind-hearted and *knew what she needed. Now and then, she met her shaggy friend on her errands. Moreover she found many new friends along the way.*

# In Search of a New Heart

*Once upon a time there was a little girl named Margaret. She loved to dance and to sing, to laugh and to skip about. She loved the flowers and the trees, the butterflies and the bees, and she enjoyed playing with the animals of the forest, in which she lived. As long as Margaret was too little to be of use to her parents, she was free to do as she pleased.*

*One day, however, her parents told her: 'It is time for you to get to know the serious side of life. Stop wasting your time with all that aimless singing, hopping and fooling around with the animals in the forest.'*

*When Margaret heard them talk like this, her heart tightened so much, that it hurt.*

*'From now on,' her mother said, 'you will keep the house clean and tidy and take care of the garden, while we go to work. And don't you dare roam about in the forest!'*

*'But I want to go and see my friends, the animals, and talk to them,' Margaret replied.*

*'Stop that nonsense at once!' her mother scolded. 'You can't speak with animals and besides, who cares, what you want?'*

*Again Margaret felt a twinge in her heart, as if it had shrunk just a tiny bit.*

Since she loved her parents and thought: 'They mean well', she did as she was told. When her parents went off for work, she tended house and garden. And often her animal-friends came by to play with her.

Again and again her parents urged her not to waste time, but to keep busy with her chores. The harder Margaret worked, the more chores her parents gave her. Never ever were they satisfied – never ever could she meet their growing demands. Every time she was scolded, Margaret felt her heart shrink a tiny bit, until in the end it was totally shriveled.

Years later – Margaret had grown up to be a young woman – the young men of her neighborhood started to court her. But as soon as they came close, they saw the big hole in the place, where her heart should have been, and turned away from her. People in the near-by village began to gossip about the 'Woman without a Heart' and soon nobody showed up anymore.

Her parents put the blame on her and chided her: 'You are a good-for-nothing – not even suited for marriage!'

On hearing this, Margaret ran away from home and fled sobbing into the forest, which had long since become unfamiliar to her. She hadn't been permitted to go there anymore, for otherwise she would not have been able to finish her chores in house and garden.

Far and far she went, without paying attention to the path, ever further into the forest. And she asked herself, how she could fill the hole in place of her heart. Finally, she sank down exhaustedly at the bottom of a rock.

A fox came by, saw her desperation, and asked her: 'You look troubled. What do you need?'

'I need a new heart!' Margaret exclaimed.

'Well, if that is all,' the fox replied, 'I can help you: Just climb this rock. On top there is an eagle's nest. Lift it and you will find, what you are looking for there.'

Reluctantly Margaret followed the advice of the fox and climbed the rock with great effort. As promised, she found the nest there. It was uninhabited. She lifted it and found a heart of flint beneath it. It fit the hole perfectly, where her heart had once been. When she had thus closed the hole, she returned home.

But people discovered pretty soon, that something was still wrong with her. Since Margaret, with her heart of flint, had a hard time empathizing with others, she was often considered insensitive. Consequently people continued to avoid her.

So she fled into the forest once more. When she had gone quite a ways, she suddenly saw something sparkle in the moss. She drew nearer and found a heart of glass, exactly the size of her flinty heart. Since the latter had not served her well, she exchanged it for the heart of glass and once again started back for home.

Now, that all people could see, what was in her heart, they did not want anything to do with her more than ever before, as they could now instantly recognize her dark, as well as her bright side. Since some of them treated her heart of glass in a very careless manner, it finally shattered into thousands of pieces. Thus she had to flee again.

Desolate she sat down under a tree. Thereon sat a raven, who asked her: 'What's bothering you?'

'Nobody loves me, because my heart is shriveled and I cannot find anything to replace it,' Margaret complained.

'To recover your heart, you will have to swim the 'Ocean of Tears'. On its bottom, you will find, what you are searching for,' the raven advised her.

'How do I get there?' Margaret inquired.

'Go through this forest, until you reach the neighboring arid plain. There you will see a high crystal mountain, which will give you the direction to the 'Ocean of Tears'.'

So Margaret walked through the dark forest, until the trees thinned out and she arrived at the arid plain, as the raven had told her. Many days and nights she was on the move, always heading towards the crystal mountain. The plain seemed to be endless.

When she was just about to give up hope, she caught sight of the first waves of the 'Ocean of Tears'. She bravely threw herself in. The waves were washing over her and almost crushed her, but she would not give up. She took a last deep breath and dived.

Deeper and deeper she dived, when suddenly she saw something glint below. When she came close, she discovered, that it was a heart of gold. She grabbed the heart, and took it with her to the surface. There she inserted it into the hole, which her broken heart had left, and returned home once again.

From now on she was welcomed by people, for she was always caring for others and forgot about herself. Everyone admired her heart of gold. She was grateful to be admitted among people again, and was able to help many of them with her diligence and her talents. And yet she felt, she was lacking something.

One day, when she was resting at the fountain of the village, a young journeyman named Gabriel passed by on his travels. Like all others, he was fascinated with her golden heart, but he also saw, that she was sad.

'What is the matter with you?' he asked her.

'Nothing!' she answered and turned away.

But he would not be fooled and sat down beside her: 'Why are you so sad then?'

She burst out: 'Because my heart is missing! That which I have is only a substitute, even if it is made of gold. I used to be able to dance, to sing, to laugh and to love, but now my heart is empty.'

'What happened?' Gabriel inquired.

'I really don't know,' Margaret answered. 'I used to have a heart like everybody else. But then it shriveled, until it was almost gone.'

'Come along!' Gabriel exclaimed. 'We shall go into the forest to see the wise owl and ask her advice.'

'I don't want to cause you any trouble,' Margaret objected timidly.

'An important matter such as this is well worth any trouble!' Gabriel replied. So they set off.

As expected, the owl knew what to do: 'If you travel a day's journey deeper into the forest, you will find a hut with a weaving loom inside. Thereon weave a cloth together and bring it to me.'

The two started at once. As night fell, they reached the hut, which was illuminated from within. Through the window they saw an old lady sitting inside and weaving.

'Come on in,' the old lady addressed them, without interrupting her work.

Bashfully, they entered. They greeted and Gabriel wanted to make their request, but the old lady interrupted him: 'I know, why you have come. But if you want to use the weaving loom, you have to give me the heart of gold.'

'But then I shall again be without a heart!' Margaret sighed.

'I will just give you a part of my own heart,' Gabriel consoled her. The old lady smiled. No sooner did she hold the golden heart in her hands, than she disappeared.

Gabriel and Margaret sat down at the weaving loom and, swift as the wind, the weaving shuttle moved back and forth between them. They looked each other into the eyes full of love and with each thread they wove, their bond grew stronger. In no time at all they had woven a gorgeous cloth. Happy and exhausted, they finally fell asleep side by side.

The next day they returned to the owl with their precious cloth.

'How do you feel?' the owl asked the young woman.

Margaret paused for a moment and grasped at her heart. 'How is this possible?' she whispered awestruck. 'I have a living, feeling heart again!'

'Yes,' the owl explained, 'nothing but the love of another person could cause you to grow a genuine heart *again. The weaving of that cloth only served to give it time to grow. If you wish, the hut and the weaving loom are yours. You can continue to weave cloths and sell them in the village.'*

*This they did and lived together happily ever after.*

# Aliens Weep Not

*There was once a young woman named Lydia. While she was leisurely strolling home from work one day, she was suddenly unobtrusively followed by a dog. When she detected him, she had to keep looking at him, for he was extremely beautiful. She glanced around to see, to whom the gorgeous animal might belong, but there was no one around. 'Are you lost?' she asked the dog. He looked up at her.*

*'Take me along!' his eyes seemed to say.*

*'I cannot take you with me. My apartment is much too small for such a big animal,' she told him, while she patted him, 'and somebody is going to miss you!'*

*But the dog kept close to her, when she continued on her way. 'Okay,' she finally gave in, 'come along! I will try to find out, who you belong to.'*

*No sooner had they entered her apartment, than the dog suddenly started to speak: 'Do not be afraid, dear Lydia, I have not come to you by chance.'*

*Of course she was afraid anyhow and looked around, whether there was anyone else in the apartment. But it was definitely the dog, who had spoken.*

*'You have nothing to fear,' he reassured her. 'I will not harm you. And I am not a dog either. I have only assumed this form on your behalf, because it is familiar to you.'*

'And what are you really?' Lydia asked warily – not sure, if she genuinely wanted to know.

'I come from a planet out of the star system you call 'Alpha Centauri', at about four light years distance from your sun,' was the answer.

'You mean, you are an extraterrestrial?' Lydia stammered and swallowed.

'Yes, but you needn't worry. I just wanted to take the opportunity to talk to a human. We would like to get to know humanity better. If you wish, I will retain this form. Thus I could move around on Earth, too, without attracting attention. May I stay with you?' the dog requested.

'Oh, but I don't know at all what you need. I have no food for you and how do I explain you to my neighbors and friends?' Lydia uttered insecurely.

'You simply tell them that I am a stray dog, which you found. I will only speak to you, if we are among ourselves,' the dog promised. 'I need no nourishment as you define it – the energy of your sun is sufficient for me.'

'What's your name?' Lydia's curiosity got the better of her.

'You couldn't pronounce my name. Why don't you just call me 'Alpha'?' the dog suggested.

In the evening Lydia wanted to visit friends.

'Take me along!' Alpha shouted excitedly.

Lydia hesitated: 'This could be a problem – they do not believe in extraterrestrials.'

'It doesn't matter. I will simply meet them as a dog. Only, if they are ready for it, will I reveal my true nature,' Alpha replied. Lydia accepted and took him along.

When they arrived at her friends' house, the whole family was sitting around the table playing a game. When the children saw the dog Lydia had brought, they immediately ran towards him.

'Oh, what a beautiful dog!' they exclaimed. 'Where did you get it?'

'I found it. It's a stray,' Lydia answered.

'Will you keep him?' they inquired.

'I don't think so,' Lydia said. 'What are you playing?'

'Come and sit down with us,' their father invited her. 'We are playing a game, in which the players must, with skill and luck, make the best of a starter cash that is the same for each.'

Lydia watched the game for some time. The father seemed to win, while the youngest child was about to lose. When he had no money left and was supposed to go to jail, he began to weep. 'No reason to shed tears – it's only a game!' his father tried to console him. But the child kept weeping.

*Finally Lydia commented: 'The objective of the game rather seems to be to finish the others off and ruin them. Do you enjoy that?'*

*'That is simplified very much!' the father countered. 'The objective is to skillfully trade, plan and do business.'*

*'But at the expense of the other players!' Lydia insisted.*

*'Well, just like in real life!' the mother remarked.*

*'Why do you train your children in a behavior that you wouldn't approve of in 'real life'? You teach them that there always must be winners and losers, don't you?' Lydia protested.*

*'That's the way it is. They will have to cope with these things later on,' the father replied.*

*'No wonder our society is as it is, if everybody is taught that they have to live at the expense of others to be a winner!' Lydia objected. 'There are certainly more reasonable patterns of behavior. Why don't we try and practice ways, in which all involved can be winners?'*

*Alpha nudged her with his snout.*

*'What do you think,' Lydia asked tentatively, 'how extraterrestrials would evaluate our behavior, if they were observing Earth?'*

'That would depend on their system of values,' the father answered. 'Do you assume that extraterrestrials are automatically the better people?'

'I don't know,' Lydia admitted.

'Besides,' the father continued, 'I don't believe that there is intelligent life on other planets.'

'Well,' Lydia smiled, 'if this vast universe with its countless galaxies, if even our Milky Way with its billions of suns contained only one single planet harboring intelligent life, that would be an enormous waste of space, wouldn't it?'

They continued their discussion for quite some time without reaching a conclusion, but Lydia kept her secret to herself. Finally she went home with Alpha.

When they arrived, Alpha, without touching upon the discussion, requested: 'The game they were playing – can you explain it to me?'

'It is about money – always just money, as is so often the case in our society!' Lydia sighed.

'What is money?' Alpha wanted to know.

'Money,' Lydia explained, 'is really a worthless piece of paper or metal, which has a value imprinted on it, so that people, in the expectation that others do likewise, give away something accordingly valuable that belongs to them.'

'Doesn't everything belong to everybody?' Alpha asked surprised.

'No,' Lydia replied, 'there are people, who own a lot and people, who own little or nothing. That's why there is so much dispute – sometimes even war – about things that are particularly valuable or scarce. Is it different where you come from?'

'Yes! We have no wars,' Alpha said, 'for where I live, nobody owns anything all by himself, because we share everything and would simply give anybody, what he seemed to need so much, that he would even use force to take it. There is enough of everything for everybody.'

'Some people say, that on Earth, too, all resources and food would be plentiful for everybody, if they were divided properly. They were sufficient for everybody's needs, but not sufficient for everybody's greed,' Lydia mused.

'What is greed?' Alpha inquired.

'Greed,' Lydia explicated, 'is like an enormous, insatiable hunger for more: more money, more power, more of everything. The result is, that a very few live at the expense of all the rest. I believe, that greed originates from a feeling of insecurity and deprivation. Basically it is probably a deep-seated hunger for love.'

'If you know the cause, why is greed still a problem?' Alpha wondered.

Lydia explained sadly: 'This problem develops again and again. Today's greedy people are yesterday's unloved children. They didn't receive the affection and emotional security that are necessary for a life lived with love. Such people often try to fill the emptiness in their hearts with material treasures throughout their lives, which obviously cannot succeed. They pass on this emptiness to the next generation. Do you not have this problem?'

'Greed, as you describe it, is unknown to us,' Alpha answered, 'since where I live, everybody gets, what they need. Nobody would take more than his fair share. Nobody in our world lives at the expense of others.'

'That sounds like a dream: no greed, no wars. Aren't there any aggressive beings, where you live?' Lydia inquired.

'No,' Alpha stated, 'in truly advanced civilizations, in addition to the development of technology, there is always a spiritual development towards love and wisdom, as well. A civilization, whose technology had developed faster than their spirits, would long since have destroyed itself. Beings that have progressed far enough to travel in space, must also be advanced enough to have overcome war and aggression – otherwise they wouldn't have survived.'

'That makes sense to me,' Lydia said pensively. 'And yet, humans always depict extraterrestrials as monsters or other aggressive beings. That's why they are often scared of them.'

'Why do they depict them in ways that scare them?' Alpha asked.

'Benevolent extraterrestrials are considered boring – only aggressive ones are interesting. Furthermore humans are often aggressive themselves and don't know, that there are other ways, that it is possible to live in peace and harmony with each other,' Lydia replied.

'Well, how could they know this, if they consider good examples boring?' Alpha reflected. 'But let's get back to that game: The child didn't seem happy during the game.'

'No,' Lydia confirmed, 'he was weeping, because he lost.'

'Is it called 'weeping', when there is water dripping out of the eyes?' Alpha wanted to know.

'Don't you ever weep?' Lydia asked incredulously. 'Or put another way: Are your people never unhappy?'

'None of us would ever force anything on anybody else, which this person wouldn't agree to. The child was not losing voluntarily, was he?' Alpha tried to understand.

'No, but he voluntarily played this game. And as in almost every game that humans play with each other, and as in real life, there are unfortunately always winners and losers. In our society both belong together. For one person to be able to win, others have to lose. It probably need not be that way,' Lydia mused.

'Basically, you do seem to know exactly, how your world would have to be organized to benefit everyone and yet you obviously act against your insights time and again and do things that don't work,' Alpha remarked thoughtfully.

'What do mean by that?' Lydia was confused.

'It is really pretty simple.' Alpha seemed to be smiling. 'If you want to live your lives in peace, joy and love, as we do, you shouldn't force anything on anyone against his will. You do cause your misery yourselves.'

'I cannot imagine, how a society would function, in which nobody was ever forced to do anything, he didn't want to,' Lydia reflected. 'That would mean, everyone only does, what he likes!'

'Precisely!' Alpha confirmed. 'Everyone does his best of his own accord, where his strengths are, and is encouraged and supported therein. Thus everybody enjoys doing their jobs, they do them well for the benefit of all and there are no losers.'

'And who does the work nobody likes, if everyone only does, what they enjoy?' Lydia questioned.

'For every necessary work, there is somebody, who is capable of it and finds fulfilment in doing it. If that were not the case, this work wouldn't be done at all, but another solution would be found,' Alpha explained.

'And that works?' Lydia was skeptical. 'What if somebody cannot or will not work?'

'I think, we have a different understanding of the term 'work'. In our society everyone contributes in some way or another to the common good. In this sense everyone 'works'. Nobody would deliberately cause harm to the others, for we all know, that what harms one person, harms all, and what doesn't benefit many, doesn't benefit any. We are all closely linked with each other.'

'That sounds, as if you were living in paradise,' Lydia marveled. 'Why do you visit Earth, if you are so far more progressed than mankind, and if we make so many mistakes?'

'We learn a lot from young civilizations, too, and humans are very inventive and imaginative. It is a pity, though, that they obviously use these special gifts in a very deficient way up to now. And yet, we recognize promising developments in Earth's humans,' Alpha rejoined.

'Couldn't you help us, to use our creativity in more reasonable ways?' Lydia begged.

'We are not allowed to interfere in the development of other civilizations,' Alpha answered determined, but Lydia retorted: 'Even if they were in danger of destroying themselves?'

Alpha reassured her: 'We see, that mankind is progressing and maturing. So we do not believe, that you will destroy yourselves, but expect you to soon reach the next level of a more peaceful coexistence.'

Suddenly he seemed to listen inwards: 'Oh, my friends are calling me. I will have to leave you. We will be gathering and flying back. I thank you very much for the new insights that you have given to me. There is a lot I will have to think about.'

Lydia became almost a bit wistful:

'Will we meet again? Do you often come to Earth?'

'Dear Lydia,' Alpha made his farewell, 'if you so wish, we can gladly meet again, soon. I have very much enjoyed your company. Perhaps, we may even be able to appear in our proper form, if you are ready for it. See you again.' And he left into the darkness.

# The Veil of Adulthood

*There were once two children, named Diana and Nico, who went through thick and thin together. They enjoyed roaming the woods and fields around their village.*

*They loved it, when the bunnies played at their feet. The birds would sit on their hands and chirp their most beautiful melodies. The butterflies danced up and down and the squirrels romped around them cheerfully. The children consulted with the wise old trees on the important issues of their lives and delighted in the teasing of the nature beings. They liked it, when the wind ruffled their hair, and it also knew all kinds of fun games.*

*For hours and hours, they would forget about everything else, when they were out in nature. Not before the church bells rang in the evenings, did they think of home again, and hurriedly returned, knowing that their parents were waiting for them with dinner.*

*Diana's parents were delighted, when she came home and told them about her adventures.*

*Nico's father, however, was very strict. He worked a lot and was habitually ill-tempered, so there was often a depressed mood at the dinner table. Not until his father had retired with his newspaper, could Nico tell his mother everything, he had experienced during the day.*

She believed him, when he described, how Diana and he talked to the trees and the animals, how they teased each other and the nature beings in the forest, and played with the wind.

His father failed to understand such "nonsense". He snorted contemptuously at such a "waste of time" and chided the mother for taking Nico's stories seriously. He was planning to introduce Nico to "real life" soon!

When Nico told Diana about this, her heart sank:

'If your father shows you "real life", I will lose you. You will forget, who you are and what is really important. Just like your father!'

'I will never become like my father!' Nico exclaimed with utter conviction. 'When I go to work with my father, I will return to you right afterwards, and we will continue to share many adventures. Don't worry! We will always stay together!'

But Diana was brokenhearted:

'Promise, that you will never forget, what we have experienced together.'

Nico smiled at her encouragingly: 'I promise!'

After that, neither of them spoke about it anymore. The days trickled by, and some time elapsed.

Then the Big Day came: His father took Nico to the factory for the first time. In the evening, he enthusiastically told Diana about the large halls full of machines, the many people and the various interesting things, that were manufactured there. Diana listened intently. It was a new and fascinating world.

After that, they turned back to their games. But something had changed. Nico soon began to get bored and make disparaging remarks, which made Diana very sad.

And it wasn't long, before he stopped coming to her regularly. When she asked about him, he increasingly found excuses, and often he was simply too tired from work.

So Diana mostly went into the woods alone, now. The trees whispered to her:

'Don't be sad. Everything will come back. You, too, will walk the path of forgetfulness. But one day you will remember. We will be waiting for you.'

Soon she was old enough to give her mother a hand in the house and garden, and she enjoyed it. Thus the door to the experiences of childhood gradually closed, and other matters became more important.

The young people of the village met for socializing and dancing, and soon one of the young men proposed to her. Before long, they moved into a home of their own. Their first child was born, and the days were filled with duties and joys, that left little time for leisure.

*Diana enjoyed caring for her family, and soon her children were roaming the woods and fields, telling of their adventures. She was amazed at their vivid imagination, but the chambers to the wonders of her own childhood remained closed to her.*

*Nico did not fare any better. He moved to the city, where there was better paid work, but this cost him all the time and energy he could muster, because he, too, had a family to support. So the two lost sight of each other.*

*The years passed and their children started their own families.*

*Now, when Diana watched her grandchildren playing in the woods, talking to invisible friends and trying to catch the wind, when she then dozed off under one of the old trees, she had the impression of hearing a murmur in their rustle: 'Remember!'*

*The thought crossed her mind: 'What if it were real, what the kids are experiencing?'*

*More and more, her heart opened again to the world of childhood wonders. What she had dismissed as "vivid imagination" before, seemed to become increasingly real to her.*

*The more time she took for leisure, for rest and contemplation, the more she began to discover another, new world, behind the busy world of the everyday hustle and bustle, that enchanted her.*

She began to think of the nature beings again, and sometimes she thought, she could feel something or someone near her, even though she could not see anything.

During this time Nico's father died, and thus she saw Nico, who returned to the village for his father's funeral, again, after a long, long time. His eyes had a dull expression and his shoulders were stooped, as if he were carrying a heavy load. She was shocked, to see him like that.

But she didn't let it show, and instead greeted him joyfully. His reaction was restrained. He looked tired.

'Are you still working at the factory?' she asked him sympathetically.

'Yes – for the moment,' he answered gloomily. 'They are about to replace me by a robot.'

'Oh dear!' Diana thought to herself, 'You almost resemble a robot yourself!'

Aloud she said: 'Wouldn't you like to go into the woods again with me sometime? You know - like we used to?'

He hesitated. No, he didn't feel like it at all, but he didn't want to hurt her.

Enthusiastically, she continued: 'I will prepare a picnic basket for us and we will have a nice time there. I am sure, you could use a little rest.'

Since it seemed to be very important to her, he reluctantly agreed in the end.

They picnicked on a blanket and he leaned with his back against one of the old trees. He watched Diana: She looked beautiful, even if life had left its marks on her face. Her cheerfulness and loving nature made her look very young. Her joyful reminiscing was contagious, and a deep longing for a more idyllic world was sparked in him.

He felt exhausted and drained. Wouldn't it be nice to pick up, where they had left so long ago? He leaned his head against the tree, let his mind wander and dozed. The wind ruffled his hair and the trees whispered to him: 'Don't you remember? There was more to life...'

Soon he was fast asleep and began to dream: His father was coming toward him across a colorful meadow of flowers, looking at him lovingly.

'Nico!' he said, 'I was a fool! Don't make the same mistake I made! You cannot take anything with you, except the love you gave to others. Turn back to what you once knew, and remember to live - your life, not mine! Take care.'

The dream was so vivid and clear, that Nico had to tell it to Diana. She looked at him in silence.

'Do you think, it was a message?' Nico asked. Diana nodded.

This message remained on Nico's mind for a long time. So when he actually lost his job to a robot, he and his wife moved back to his parents' house to live with his mother.

The atmosphere of the village felt good to him – better than the hustle and bustle of the city. His wife became friends with Diana and they spent a lot of time together with their children and grandchildren. Nico now got to know life from an entirely different perspective. He was never without work. When he wasn't busy in his own house and garden, he went to assist his mother or his neighbors.

Also, he often went for walks now, alone or with others, in the fields and woods, and enjoyed not having to function, but simply to be. Only now did he realize, how much he had felt enslaved by the fixed rhythm, to which he had been subjected in his work. He had lived completely against his nature.

He became fond of listening to Diana, his wife and the children telling him, what was important to them. That would never have occurred to him until then.

His dream brought him back to the wellsprings of joy and fulfillment, and he was extremely grateful to Diana and his wife for sharing their experiences with him and taking an interest in his.

He felt younger and more alive with each passing day and was amazed at himself.

*Diana observed, how Niko interacted with the little ones, and how much he enjoyed their games. She felt him becoming increasingly peaceful and calm, and opening up more and more to his surroundings. Soon they felt their old bond again.*

*The more time they spent with the children, the more they became involved in their games and their world, the more they felt an inkling, that perhaps not everything they were talking about, was pure fantasy. And they wondered: 'What if it were real, what the kids are experiencing?'*

*So they came full circle after all those years, and returned to the inner knowledge, they had possessed as children.*

# An Exceptional Warfare

*Once upon a time there were two kings, who could not possibly have been more contrasting: King Heinous was cold and calculating, wanting to be in control of everything, trusting nobody but himself and always discontented. His coat of arms showed a sword.*

*King Wiseman, on the other hand, was warmhearted, gentle and trusting and at one with himself. His blazonry was a flower.*

*In King Heinous' kingdom fear and terror dominated among the subjects, for he ruled the land with a rod of iron. He tried to press as many taxes and duties from his subjects as possible, so that they could hardly make a living. His henchmen controlled everything and everybody and they often lashed and imprisoned people, who did not obey their orders or rebelled against injustices. His subjects distrusted each other, for they could never be sure, if their neighbor didn't spy for King Heinous and would betray and turn them in to him. Their lives were harsh and full of deprivation.*

*King Heinous fought many wars, since he could just never get enough.*

*King Wiseman, on the other hand, always tried to live in peace with everyone. His subjects trusted him implicitly. When he issued orders, they were clear and* easily comprehensible, so that everyone knew, what was expected of him. He never demanded too much of anybody and always tried to employ people according to their abilities. In his kingdom love and mutual respect dominated. His subjects voluntarily paid him tithes of their crops, so that the King's court was well supplied. The King put part of it into storage for times of famine. Nobody suffered want.

The neighboring kingdom had long since been a thorn in King Heinous' side. He envied King Wiseman for his fertile fields, meadows and woods, which were cultivated in close communion with nature. King Heinous' fields performed poorly in comparison, since his peasants often had to go off to war, and therefore couldn't sow and grow enough crops.

Thus, one day King Heinous decided to conquer the neighboring kingdom and declared war on King Wiseman without further ado. Yet, when he arrived at the battlefield with his army bristling with weapons, he found nothing and nobody there. King Wiseman had simply not showed up.

King Heinous suspected an ambush and sent out scouts to track down King Wiseman's army. The scouts searched the surroundings for one day, even a second day, only to come back to King Heinous without having achieved anything. There simply wasn't anybody to be found.

King Heinous boiled with rage. 'If he doesn't come to us, we'll go and get him!' he shouted and set his army into motion. They were on the move for three days and nights, since they didn't dare set up a camp for fear of an ambush. The villages and towns, which they passed, however, seemed empty.

Finally, they reached the Royal City. Everywhere on the battlement of the city wall, there were cheering people throwing down flowers.

'This is a trap!' King Heinous, who was riding ahead of his army, shouted. 'Spread out!' Thus the army surrounded the whole city wall.

'Welcome!' King Wiseman shouted down from the watchtower. Cautiously King Heinous rode towards the city gate. When he entered the gate – what did he see?

He looked into countless mirrors! The sunlight was reflected by all those mirrors and he instinctively raised his arm to protect his eyes. The trumpeter of his army took this to be the sign for the retreat and gave the signal. The whole large army withdrew.

Friendly hands helped the dazzled and dazed king off his horse and the city gate was closed, before King Heinous could resolve the error.

'Brother', said King Wiseman, who had meanwhile descended from the tower, 'be our guest.'

'I am at your mercy,' King Heinous answered with clenched teeth, when he realized his situation. Without his army, he was a Nobody. They had obediently retreated in the meantime.

Soon, he was surrounded by cheering people, though, who threw flowers on his path. King Wiseman put a wreath of flowers around his neck. 'You are welcome!' he said smiling. 'Let's talk.'

The talks lasted several days. What the two discussed, nobody ever came to know. Fact is, that King Heinous returned to his kingdom a few days later, changed and chastened, accompanied by a delegation of King Wiseman, which was to help him set up a new and better order in his Kingdom.

It was very difficult to convince his subjects of the change of mind of King Heinous. They had been suffering under his tyranny for too long. But the two kings kept in close contact with each other from now on, and there was an active exchange of the subjects of both kingdoms.

The peasants in King Heinous' kingdom didn't have to go to war anymore and could thus cultivate their fields, so that nobody had to suffer want anymore.

Over time the subjects' trust in each other grew again and they also started to trust King Heinous. Rarely were there relapses into old habits, which were always corrected gently.

*It thus happened that King Wiseman's exceptional warfare came to be a blessing for all. Again the old saying proved to be true:*

*'A soft answer turneth away wrath'.*

# Brother Death and Sister Life

*On a fine summer morning, Death and his sister Life went for a walk, taking time to plan their assignments for the day. When they were through, Life said to her brother Death: 'It is really a pity that people perceive us so differently. Very few understand, that we are actually doing the same kind of work: We help them with their birth into a new existence.'*

*'Yes,' Death replied, 'they will always believe that you do and embrace you for it, but I am pushed off and rejected. That really isn't fair! They think I were their enemy.'*

*'Still people ultimately do not understand either of us!' Life remarked. 'If they knew, how to deal with their existence, you, my brother, would be the highlight of their lives – not the fall into nowhere. It is often said: 'If you are afraid of death, you are also afraid of life', which means: Those who reject you, really reject both of us. Unfortunately, only a very few still know, that the art of dying is also the art of living, which has to be learned in time.'*

*'True!' Death confirmed. 'Most people try not to think of me, until I stand in front of them – that's too late to give their lives meaning or to check if the course is right. Many people tend to speed up, just when they have lost sight of their goal, their dreams.'*

They had arrived at the place of their first assignment, coming to a 42-year-old man, who lay in hospital after a motorcycle-accident. When he saw Death approaching, he started to cry:

'If I had only taken more time for my family! I have led a life on the fast lane and valued nothing but money, power and success. My work has always been more important to me, than everything else. If I had only taken more time to love, to laugh and to dance. I wish, I could get another chance!'

Life took his hand and placed it in the hand of her brother Death: 'It is too late!'

Their next assignment brought them to a woman in her mid-fifties. She, too, began to lament at the sight of Death:

'All my life I have only been there for others and have always read their every wishes from their eyes. Never did I ever ask anything for myself! Why do I have to go already – now, that I finally have time for myself?'

'You have neglected to listen to your heart,' Death answered, 'although it is the compass to what you had originally wanted to achieve with your existence. If you had led your life more in accordance with your talents and needs, instead of adapting to the expectations – or even just the supposed expectations – of others, I could now escort you fulfilled and peaceful to the Other Side.'

'Yes, in the hustle and bustle of everyday life I have often failed to listen to my soft inner voice, I admit, but haven't I done a lot of good?' the woman replied.

'You have indeed,' Life confirmed, 'but your body has warned you again and again, that you lived contrary to your needs. You didn't heed its signals. It is now time to leave.'

With this Life took her hand and placed it in the hand of her brother Death.

On the way to their next assignment Life said: 'What could we do, to make it easier for people to be more conscious of both of us, so that they would start thinking about us before you stand in front of them?'

'Scare them!' Death exclaimed and grinned mischievously. 'Simply fire warning shots across theirs bows every now and then.'

'Isn't there a more gentle way?' his sister reflected. 'What, if we worked together more closely? If you picked people up and returned them to me, they could tell the living of the existence you took them to. Then everybody would know, that they have nothing to fear – neither in life nor in death – if they observe a very few rules. In any case, they would then understand that there won't be nothingness awaiting them, when you come for them!'

'We have been trying that time and again!' Death objected. 'They simply didn't believe the returnees – not even the religious people did, who should have an interest in their reports, since they cover their very own field of expertise and confirm their teachings.'

'Well,' Life pointed out, 'some religious institutions might be afraid to lose their power, if there were a steady flow of witnesses coming back from the hereafter and their 'flock' consequently lost fear of it.'

'There really is no reason, either, for them to be frightened of the world beyond their perception – just to have respect! For as all wisdom teachings confirm: 'As you sow, so shall you reap!' To reap love, you have to plant it!' Death emphasized. 'Each decision someone makes, either moves him towards love or away from it. And the sum total of these decisions makes up the condition, in which the person leaves.'

'In their heart of hearts,' Life said, 'people all know this, but their fear keeps them from following the path of their hearts.'

'But what are they so afraid of, and why?' Death inquired.

'They fear not to belong anymore,' Life answered. 'They have been taught, it were selfish to listen inwards, that only the authorities knew, what was good for them, and if people didn't comply with the authorities' goals and wishes, they fear to be excluded from society. So they get into a conflict between inner and outer voices and the greater the conflict, the greater their fear to stay alone.

They ought to be reconnected to the Source of Love – the One Source of All Being, so that they would know again, that they are never alone. That is the original mission of religion. People would have to be convinced again, that they are loved unconditionally, that God doesn't expect them to qualify by good conduct of any sort. The only thing He requires, is trust. The separation they feel would be eliminated at once and all anxiousness become unnecessary.'

'But when I come,' Death pointed out, 'the separation is eliminated anyway and everyone returns to the Source – as close to Love and Light as he wishes or can bear. If you have spent your life in darkness, you will keep a greater distance than someone who has always been open to the Light. And yet, there will be no separation anymore, for God is all and in all. People have to decide for themselves, whether they want to wait until I come, to reconnect to the Source.'

'You are quite right,' Life conceded, 'we shouldn't interfere. The only thing I would like to get across is, that we want to be people's friends – not foes. I hope, we will succeed one day.'

Finally they came to a 94-year-old lady. She, too, lay in bed. When she saw Death approaching, her face lit up.

'Are you coming for me at last?' she asked smiling.

'Do you not fear me?' Death inquired.

'No!' she answered. 'I have had a fulfilled life. It has not always been easy, but I have walked my path and have had many wonderful experiences. The hardships, too, ultimately served their purpose, for they helped me learn love and compassion and not to become too arrogant.'

'Are you ready then to come with me?' Death asked.

'With all my heart!' the old lady answered him.

Life helped her to sit up, took her hand and placed it in the hand of her brother Death. The lady took Death's hand, embraced him and danced with him out of the room.

Flower of Life

# Meaning of the Names

(in the order of their appearance)

| | | |
|---|---|---|
| 1. | *Ella* | Different |
| 2. | *Benedict* | Blessed |
| 3. | *Liora* | God is my Light |
| 4. | *Raja* | Hope |
| 5. | *Yelina* | Light |
| 6. | *Jason* | Healer |
| 7. | *Daria* | God's Gift |
| 8. | *Sophia* | Wisdom |
| 9. | *Philo* | Friend |
| 10. | *Elisa* | My God is Abundance |
| 11. | *Margaret* | Pearl |
| 12. | *Gabriel* | Man of God |
| 13. | *Lydia* | = *First European Christian* |
| 14. | *Diana* | Divine |
| 15. | *Nico* | Victory |